ALFIE
~ THE ~
WEREWOLF

More books in the series

Birthday Surprise
Full Moon
Silvertooth
Wolf Wood
Werewolf Secrets

ALFIE THE WEREWOLF
The Evil Triplets

Written by
Paul van Loon

Translated by
David Colmer

Illustrated by
Hugo van Look

Hodder
Children's
Books

A division of Hachette Children's Books

First published in The Netherlands under the title *Weerwolvenbos*
by Uitgeverij Leopold in 2005
Published by arrangement with Rights People, London

First published in Great Britain in 2011 by Hodder Children's Books

The publishers are grateful for the support of the
Dutch Foundation for Literature.

1

A Catalogue record for this book is available from the British Library

ISBN 978 0 340 98982 1

Typeset in Weiss by Avon DataSet Ltd,
Bidford on Avon, Warwickshire

Printed and bound in Great Britain by
CPI Bookmarque Ltd, Croydon, Surrey

The paper and board used in this paperback by Hodder Children's Books
are natural recyclable products made from wood grown in
sustainable forests. The manufacturing processes conform to the
environmental regulations of the country of origin.

Hodder Children's Books
a division of Hachette Children's Books
338 Euston Road, London NW1 3BH
An Hachette UK Company
www.hachette.co.uk

For Hadjidja

1

Cackle, cackle

'*Wrow*, what a beautiful moon.'

Alfie the Werewolf walked out of the garden and on to the street, swishing his tail with longing. It was midnight and everyone was asleep. The light of the full moon reflected off his glasses.

'*Wrow*, fantastic,' Alfie growled. 'I get to be a wolf again. For three nights in a row.' He howled happily at the moon – '*Wrow-a-woo*' – then ran round the corner.

Suddenly he was in a dark alley where there was no moonlight and no streetlights.

'Hey, werewolf!' A strange voice came out of the darkness. Eyes gleamed.

'*Wrow*, who's that?'

No reply.

In the darkness something moved, something very big. Alfie stayed where he was.

'C-come out,' he growled. 'If you d-d-dare.'

The voice gave a cackling laugh. 'Are you scared? You chicken killer.'

Alfie took a step back.

'I-I'm not scared. I'm a w-w-werewolf. Very dangerous. Listen, *wrow*.'

The growl that came out of his throat was very quiet. It was the growl of a mouse. Not much more than a squeak.

Quickly he took another step back, then another, until he was in the moonlight again. That felt safer.

Slowly, something emerged from the dark alley. Alfie's jaw dropped. It was white. And it had feathers, cold eyes and a beak. And big, clawed yellow feet.

Alfie gulped when its shadow fell over

him. He rubbed his eyes with his paws.

Standing in front of him was a chicken, but no ordinary chicken. It was enormous. It was gigantic. Even bigger than Alfie's werewolf cousin, Leo. It was definitely the biggest chicken in the world. A dream come true for a fast-food restaurant.

It stalked forward menacingly.

'I'll get you,' the chicken cackled. 'I'll peck you. I'll squash you. I'll mash you to mush.'

Alfie flinched back. 'N-no,' he shouted. 'Don't. I never hurt chickens. It's been ages. I hardly even think of chicken these days.'

The chicken gave another cackling laugh. '*Broark*, you're lying, wolf. What about Mrs Chalker's chickens?'

'That was a long time ago!' Alfie exclaimed.

'Fibber!'

The sharp beak swung down like an axe at Alfie, who dived out of the way just in time.

Crack! The beak smashed a hole in the pavement.

'Stop,' Alfie shouted. 'This is impossible. Chickens can't talk.'

'Huh, look who's talking,' the chicken cluttered. 'Nothing unusual about a talking wolf, I suppose.'

Again it chopped at Alfie.

Quickly Alfie threw himself forward. The swinging beak brushed his ear.

Crack! Another broken paving stone.

'That's enough,' growled Alfie, looking up

to where the full moon was smiling at him.

'Come on, you're not a wimp, are you?' the moon said.

A growl rose up in Alfie's throat. *'Wrow!'*

His blood surged through his veins. He turned and stared at the chicken. *'Wrow*, I'm sick of this,' he growled in a rasping voice.

The chicken's beak flashed in the moonlight. Suddenly it had a skinny face and a thin, hooked nose. Mrs Chalker's face.

The Chalker chicken cackled with delight.

Alfie leapt forward. His teeth were sharp. His claws were curved. He growled and hurled himself at the chicken.

Feathers flew up in the air as the growling and cackling grew even louder. Then Alfie heard voices. They were singing a strange song.

> *'Rub, rub, rub away,*
> *Here and all about,*
> *Rubbedy, rubbedy, rubbedy, rubbedy,*
> *Rub the last one out.'*

2

Shadows

Alfie shot up. What was that song? Who were those voices?

He looked round in a daze. He was on the floor and the moon was shining into his bedroom. White feathers were scattered everywhere.

Oh no, thought Alfie. I really did fight that chicken. I must have torn it apart. What a . . .

Then he saw his duvet and pillow ripped open on the floor next to him. He looked at his hands. They were white and hairy, and his fingers ended in claws. His arms were covered with shaggy white fur.

Alfie sighed with relief. Suddenly he understood. He'd had a chicken nightmare. That was all.

Plus the full moon, of course. He'd turned into a werewolf in his sleep and ripped open his duvet and pillow. He sighed. Being able to suddenly grow claws wasn't always easy.

Then the voices reached his bedroom again.

They're real, thought Alfie, because I'm awake now.

He grabbed his glasses from the bedside table and walked over to the window. The voices sounded even louder now. They were shrill, like shrieking witches' voices.

> 'Rub, rub, rub away,
> Rub the last one out.
> Rubbedy, rubbedy, rubbedy, rubbedy,
> Gone without a doubt.'

It was a very strange song. Ominous. It sent shivers down Alfie's spine, even though he didn't understand it at all.

Cautiously he slid aside the curtain to look out. He saw the garden and the street and the houses across the road. Everything looked very different in the night-time. The houses were quiet and sleeping and full of dark shadows. Down the street was the house where Mrs Chalker used to live. Now it was as empty and dark as a haunted house.

Why on earth did I dream about Mrs Chalker? thought Alfie. Could that mean something?

He looked out over the rooftops for a moment longer. The street led off into the distance like a winding black ribbon. Somewhere beyond those roofs was Noura's house. That was a comforting thought.

Above the houses the full moon smiled at him. It was time to go out on an adventure.

Suddenly his thoughts came back to earth. Two figures were moving in the street below.

Dark shadows in the moonlight. They looked like they'd been cut out of a sheet of black paper.

Skinny, both of them. Funny hats, both of them. Umbrellas, both of them. There was something familiar about them, something familiar about both of them.

Alfie rubbed his eyes. That hat. That umbrella.

No, he thought. It can't be true! It looks like . . .

He shook his head. Impossible!

It can't be *her*. *She* was always alone. There are *two* of this one.

What's more, *she* is locked up at the RCUPA. The Reception Centre for Unusual People and Animals.

I must be sleepwalking, he thought. There's no other explanation.

For a moment Alfie hesitated. What do I do now? Then suddenly he knew.

I'll just sleepwalk right back to bed. And then tomorrow it will all have been a bad dream. Good plan!

He turned round, walked over to his bed, flopped down on it and fell asleep straightaway.

Outside the voices started again.

'*Rub, rub, rub them out,*
Rub the last one out . . .'

3

An Enormous Creature?

The yowling was deafening. Alfie shot up in bed with his hair standing on end. The noise reverberated in his stomach. It jangled through his body.

The morning sun was shining through his window. He was an ordinary boy again without fur and without claws. His duvet and pillow were lying on the floor in pieces. Mum wasn't going to be happy.

Again the hideous noise echoed through the house. It was coming from downstairs. Alfie had never heard anything like it. He rubbed his eyes, got out of bed and walked over to the door.

Tim was out on the landing, his eyes big and dark in his pale face.

'Did you hear that?' he whispered.

Alfie nodded. 'What is it?'

Tim shrugged. 'It sounds like . . . a wounded dragon or something.'

A rattling sigh came from downstairs.

'See?' Tim whispered. 'Like an enormous creature gasping for breath.'

'Or a ginormous one farting,' Alfie said. 'We'd better go and have a look.'

They stood motionless at the top of the stairs.

'Shouldn't we warn Mum and Dad?' Alfie asked.

Tim shook his head. 'I already checked their bedroom. They're not there.'

'Oh no,' said Alfie. 'Maybe they already went to look . . .'

Tim nodded. 'Come on, they might be in danger.'

Together they sneaked downstairs, the

yowling getting louder with every step they took. A heavy, squeaking sigh was coming from behind the living-room door. They exchanged glances and Tim nodded.

'OK,' Alfie said. 'I'll count to three. One, two . . . three.' Cautiously he nudged the door open. The howling blared out at them through the crack.

'You see anything?' Tim whispered.

Alfie shook his head. 'It won't open any further. Someone's in front of it.'

Suddenly it was quiet.

'Don't,' a voice pleaded. 'Please, stop.'

Horrified, Tim looked at Alfie. 'That's Mum! She's in danger.'

Alfie gave a big nod. 'Come on, let's knock the door down.'

Together they backed away for a run-up.

'Ready?' Tim said.

'Ready.'

They charged at the door and rammed into it together. *WHAM!* The door flew open . . .

4

The Green Monster

Tim and Alfie fell into the room and rolled over the floor, coming to a stop under the coffee table with Tim on top of Alfie.

'Hi, boys,' said a cheerful voice. 'Now *that* is what I call an entrance. Really unusual.'

Two familiar faces peered under the table at Tim and Alfie.

'Look who we have here,' Tim's mother said. 'Our sons.'

'Yes, I recognized them too,' said Dad.

Tim and Alfie crawled out from under the table. They looked left. They looked right.

There were no wounded dragons or any other creatures anywhere in sight. Mum looked healthy and Dad seemed to be OK too. He did have an upside-down watering can on his head. That was a bit strange. Usually he wore a tea cosy shaped like an elephant or sometimes a flowerpot. The watering can was new. He also had something strange hanging on his chest. A big green stretchy thing with lots of shiny buttons.

'What's that?' Alfie asked. 'It looks like a giant caterpillar with a control panel.'

Dad smiled at Alfie. 'How do you like my accordion? I call it the Green Monster because it's such a beautiful shade of dark green.' He stroked the instrument lovingly.

'Oh no,' Tim whispered. 'Dad's discovered music. Now I know what that howling was . . .'

'These two are real characters,' Dad said. 'They don't just walk in, they dive under the table, the jokers. That's a lot different to coming in normally. I'm going to turn it into a song. A sad song, full of woe and sorrow. A real tearjerker.'

Using both hands, he pulled the accordion out as far as it would go, then pushed it back in. A deep sigh came out of it. Dad started singing loudly. And very badly.

> 'There were two little boys,
> Poor, lonely and alone,
> No one to care about them,
> No home to call their own . . .'

His voice was as out of tune as the Green Monster. Tim and Alfie were stunned. He was singing at the top of his lungs and a tear was trickling down his cheek.

> 'They were so very hungry,
> Like hungry children in a fable,
> They had no beds, they had no roof,
> They lived under a table.
> And . . .'

The accordion was making a constant yowling sound. Tim and Alfie covered their

ears with their hands.

'William, stop!' Mum shouted. 'Don't . . .'

Dad stopped playing and looked up with surprise. The tear splashed down on the accordion.

'What's wrong?' he asked. 'Don't you think it's beautiful and touching? Even I'm moved.'

Tim and Alfie looked at each other. They didn't want to hurt Dad's feelings.

Mum coughed. 'Hmm, sweetheart, look, it's like this . . . Playing the accordion is an art and so is singing. It takes a lot of practice.'

Dad nodded. 'I know that, dear. I'll practise on my Green Monster every day. For hours! I promise.'

'Every day?' Tim groaned. 'Oh no.'

'Ugh!' said Alfie.

Dad looked at them and raised an eyebrow. 'What's the matter, boys? Have you got stomach ache or something?'

Before Tim and Alfie could answer, they heard three loud bangs in the hall. *SMACK! FLOTCH! SPLAT!*

All four of them turned their heads towards the front door. Mum had gone pale.

'What was that?' she asked.

5

Egg Attack

They all ran into the hall and Tim pulled open the front door. There was no one in sight, but three splattered eggs were slowly dripping down the front door, leaving three long yellow stripes. And R.O.W. Club had been painted on the door in ugly black letters.

For a few minutes they stared at it in astonishment.

'What's the Row Club?' Tim asked finally.

Alfie shrugged. 'Never heard of it. Maybe a club that likes to pick rows with people?'

'Shall I write a song about it?' Dad asked.

'No, maybe not,' Mum said quickly. 'Maybe they heard your accordion, dear. You were making quite a row.'

'Yeah,' Tim said. 'That must be why they threw the eggs. They think this is a row club.'

'Oh,' Dad said, looking gloomy for a moment and scratching his head under the watering can. Then his face cleared up.

'You mean . . . You think they don't like beautiful music?'

Tim, Alfie and Mum looked at each other.

Mum shook her head, so slightly it was almost imperceptible.

'It was probably just some kids messing around,' she said. 'Oh! That reminds me.'

'What of, sweetheart?' Dad asked.

Mum raised a finger in the air. 'I have to buy a new broom. A very good one.'

Alfie raised a finger too. 'Um, I need a new duvet. And a new pillow too. They're a bit torn. I had some pretty wild dreams last night.'

Mum smiled at him. 'I bet it was a wild werewolf dream, huh, son?'

'Ohhh,' Dad let out a jealous groan. 'If only *I* had wild werewolf dreams and ripped *my* pillow open.'

Tim rolled his eyes. 'OK, this is all very interesting, but are we going to have breakfast or not? Alfie and I have to go to school.'

Dad nodded. 'It's a shame though. The Row Club song would have been something special.' He shrugged. 'I'd better repaint the front door. And then I'll go and find a street corner to play my songs on.'

He went back inside and laid his accordion on the floor under the new coat rack. It was an elk-antler coat rack he'd bought at a car-boot sale. After staring at it thoughtfully for a moment, his eyes lit up. Generally that meant he'd had a brilliant idea.

'Hey, what if I had antlers on my head?' he said. 'That would be fantastic and really different. No one has antlers on their head.' He sighed. 'It would be almost as fantastic as being a werewolf. But I'll never be one of them either. I just don't have a wild existence in store for me.'

Downcast, he shuffled through to the kitchen, where a wild boiled egg was waiting for him.

6

Luke

'Someone attacked our house,' Alfie said.

'Really?' said Noura.

Noura was Alfie's friend and they sat next to each other at school. Just like him, she turned into a werewolf at full moon. A black one.

Mr French was explaining something about rhyme. He wrote some words on the blackboard: shopper, walker, orange.

'This morning,' Alfie said.

'Really?' said Noura.

Alfie noticed that she wasn't really listening

to him. She was smiling at Luke.

Luke was a new boy with shoulder-length black hair. His face always looked smooth and slightly blank, and he wore a silver earring in his left ear. Around his neck he wore a cool leather strap that looked a bit like a dog collar, and he was a very good roller-blader.

Alfie thought he was stupid. His ears stuck out and he had a strange, croaky voice. But Noura didn't seem to notice.

Alfie glanced outside for a moment. A blur passed by the window.

'What do you mean?' asked Noura.

Alfie looked at her. 'What?'

'What kind of attack?' said Noura, who must have been listening after all.

'Oh, yeah, by the Row Club,' said Alfie. 'They bombed our front door. With eggs.'

'Wow, egg terrorists,' said Noura, waving at Luke.

Mr French turned back to the class. 'So,' he said. 'Yesterday we talked about rhymes. Now I'd like you to write down as many words as you can think of that rhyme with these three words.'

Alfie sighed. 'It was probably because of Dad,' he said. 'Dad started playing the accordion all of a sudden. He's terrible.'

'Oh, that's sad,' said Noura.

'Yeah, and he sings along too.'

'That's even sadder.'

'Yeah, and his singing's even worse.'

Suddenly Alfie fell silent. He stared past Noura at the window. There were smudges and handprints all over the glass, but he could still make out a shadow outside. There was someone standing there.

'Hey, Noura, look,' Alfie whispered. 'Someone's spying on us.'

'What? Where?' Noura turned round, but there was no one there.

Alfie shook his head. 'No, it's nothing. I must have been seeing things.'

'Alfie. Noura,' Mr French called out. 'Stop gossiping. You're not writing anything down. What rhymes with walker?'

'Um, water?' said Alfie vacantly, still

peering at the window out of the corner of one eye.

Mr French smiled. 'I'm afraid not. Who knows one?'

Vincent put up his hand. 'Talker?'

'That's right,' said Mr French, writing the word on the blackboard. 'Who knows another one? If you get more than twelve, I'll buy ice creams for the whole class.'

All over the room, fingers shot up in the air.

'Squawker.'

'Stalker.'

'Hawker.'

'Keep going, keep going,' laughed Mr French, tossing a piece of chalk up and down in his hand.

Suddenly Alfie saw the shadow reappear at the window. A face pressed up against the window pane. Skinny. With a bony nose. Fierce eyes moved behind the dirty glass.

'Sir, look,' exclaimed Alfie. 'At the window.'

'Chalker!' a voice behind him cried.

1

Being Different

Alfie looked round in fright and saw Luke with his hand in the air.

'Chalker,' he said again.

'Yes, excellent, Luke,' Mr French said. 'Now you just need seven more.' He looked around the class, but no one else had any suggestions. Then he laughed. 'That was a trick question. There aren't twelve words that rhyme with walker. Mean of me, huh?'

'That's very mean,' Noura shouted.

Luke smiled at her.

When he smiles, he looks like a panting

dog, thought Alfie.

'Not fair!' the class shouted.

Alfie sighed with relief. For a moment he'd been reminded of Mrs Chalker, and just thinking of his evil neighbour sent a shiver down his spine. What would he do if she suddenly appeared in front of him? Fortunately that wasn't possible. She was safely locked away. It was just a shame that stupid Luke—

'What did you just call out, Alfie?' Mr French asked.

Alfie pointed at the window. 'Someone was standing there, sir. A peeper.'

Mr French walked over to the window, looked out and shrugged. 'I can't see anyone, Alfie. Maybe it was a lonesome tramp.' He gave a reassuring smile. 'Either way, they're gone now. What rhymes with lonesome? If you get more than twelve, I'll buy ice creams for the whole class every day for the rest of the year . . .'

Alfie walked home with Tim.

Tim was a year older than Alfie and a year above him at school. He was Alfie's best friend and Alfie lived with him too. Tim's parents had adopted Alfie and that kind of made them brothers, which they both thought was super cool. They were crazy about each other and never argued.

'What's wrong?' Tim said. 'You look so thoughtful.'

Alfie kicked a stone across the street and scratched his head hard. 'I don't know. All kinds of stuff. I've had a funny feeling lately. Last night I heard a really weird song in my dream. And there's a new kid in our class. He's called Luke. Noura likes him.'

'Oh, that's a pain!' Tim said.

Alfie nodded. 'So I think he's stupid. And just now there was a sneaky peeper outside our classroom.'

Tim laughed. 'Maybe it was Dad. Not the peeper, that song in your dream.'

'No, it was different,' Alfie said. 'Not one of those crazy songs of Dad's. The dream song was really nasty. But I've forgotten how it went.'

They crossed the road. Suddenly Tim stopped. 'Oops, hide. There he is.' He dived behind a car. 'Quick, Alfie, get down.'

Alfie didn't understand. He went over behind the car and stood next to Tim. 'What's wrong? Why do we have to hide?'

Tim pointed. 'Look. There. On the corner.'

Alfie peered along Tim's finger. Then he saw it. Someone was standing on the other side of the street on the corner. He had a big case with him and an upturned hat on the pavement in front of him. On his head he was wearing an upside-down rubber boot.

'Oh no,' Tim groaned. 'Now Dad's going to start busking. He probably thinks he's going to be discovered and end up on TV. I'm so embarrassed, I could die.'

Alfie watched

Dad strap on the Green Monster. 'It doesn't matter,' he said. 'Dad likes being different. It makes him happy.'

Tim shook his head. 'But everyone will laugh at him. When he plays, he sounds like a cat yowling. He sings like a crow. He's making a real fool of himself. And that makes me look stupid too. I'm going to pretend I don't know him.'

Alfie scratched his head. Then he scratched under his chin and behind his ears. He always got very itchy at full moon. He got itchy when he was angry too. He could feel his ears burning.

'Tim,' Alfie said. 'Listen to me! I'm a werewolf! At full moon I turn into a monster. But your dad loves me. He adopted me, with Mum. I'll never be ashamed of him. No matter how silly he acts. And I think it's really stupid of you to think like that.' Then he strode away from Tim.

He crossed the road and walked straight up to Dad.

8

Busking

Alfie's heart pounded in his chest. He felt very strange.

He'd never had an argument with Tim before, but now he was angry at him for the first time ever. What was happening?

Maybe it's because I'll turn into a werewolf again tonight, he thought. It always makes me a bit snappier than usual. But it's still stupid of Tim to be ashamed of Dad!

He took a deep breath.

He was having a very bad day.

First there was the Row Club attack. Then

a mysterious peeper. And stupid Luke, of course. And now he'd had an argument with Tim. Things couldn't get worse.

Then he had no more time to think. He'd reached the other side of the street, where Dad was standing with his accordion. 'Who wants to hear a song?' he called. 'I'm Will Friend, the folk singer. For a small donation, I'll sing a song for you.'

People hurried by without asking for a song. Some of them even sped up. There wasn't a single coin in his hat.

'Hi, Dad,' said Alfie.

Dad looked up with surprise and a big grin immediately covered his face. 'Hey, Alfie. Is school finished already? Where's Tim?'

Alfie glanced back at the car Tim was hiding behind and shrugged. 'He ... um, I think he went straight home, Dad. He had a lot of homework, I think.'

Dad smiled. 'Ah, Tim always does his best. He's a real chip off the old block. I'm proud of him. And I'm proud of you too, Alfie.'

He pulled the accordion out as far as it

went, making it wheeze like an asthmatic cow. Passers-by looked up in horror.

'Who wants a song?' Dad called. 'Get out your hankies, here it comes.'

He started singing loudly.

'Ye-hesterdayyyyy . . .'

An old man threw a coin into the hat. 'That's for you, kid,' he whispered. 'If you can get him to stop that caterwauling.' He hurried on quickly.

Dad beamed at Alfie. 'You see that, Alfie? It works. People are paying for my music.'

Alfie nodded. 'I'm going home, Dad,' he said. 'I've got homework too. And tonight . . .'

Dad smiled. 'I know, son. Full moon. Then you'll go out werewolfing. *Au-wooo* and all that. Fabulous. All that werewolf stuff's amazing. If only I could do it too.' He ruffled Alfie's hair. 'But fortunately I have other talents. I can play music. Off you go, Alfie. I'll see you later. There are people here who need entertaining.'

'See you later, Dad.'

Alfie walked off.
He didn't wait for Tim.

8

An Old Lady

Dad looked around. 'Who'd like to hear something?'

An old lady with a weird hat on her head shuffled past.

'Madam, would you like to hear a beautiful, sentimental song?' Dad asked, and started to sing.

> 'Oh, Granny, now your hair is grey,
> Remember on that sunny day . . .'

The old lady stared at him. She had a long

bony face, one eye closed tight, and a nose like a beak.

Dad studied her more closely.

'Do I know you? You look very much like someone I know. Is that you?'

The old lady shook her head.

'I very much doubt it, Mr Busker. I don't know you.'

She leant closer to Dad, sniffed him, then breathed in deeply through her nose. She seemed to think for a moment, before shaking her head softly. She brought her umbrella up and pointed it at Dad.

'You can do me a favour, boy.'

Dad gave her a broad smile. 'It would be my pleasure. What can I do for you?'

'Keep your big mouth shut,' the old lady snarled, moving the sharp silver point of her umbrella closer to Dad.

Dad took hold of the point carefully and pushed the umbrella aside. 'Don't you know that's dangerous? You shouldn't point at people with something sharp like that.'

'So I shouldn't point at people, hey, smart

alec?' the old lady said. Then she swung her umbrella at him. *WHAM!* The boot flew off Dad's head.

By the time Dad had scrambled back up on to his feet, the old lady was gone. The boot was on the ground. Dad felt his head.

'Wow, sometimes the fans get a bit *too* enthusiastic. I think I'd better go home and lie down on the sofa for a while.' He put the accordion back in its case and wobbled off down the street.

The old lady was standing in a dark doorway. She still had one eye squeezed shut and peered at Dad with the other. Then she pulled a mobile phone out of her handbag and typed in a number.

'Code 3,' she said. 'Suspicious local observed and whacked. He seems harmless enough. Wears head-boot and accordion. Does not react to silver. Probably isn't one of them. But still a weirdo.' She peered around silently for a moment. 'I went to the school too. Looked in all the classrooms. Couldn't tell which ones were and which ones weren't. Maybe they all are. All those little brats look alike. We'll have to rely on little brother.' The old lady glared at a boy who was walking past. 'What you looking at, guttersnipe? Get outta here or I'll whack you one.' She lashed out at him with the umbrella. 'Scat. Hssss. Scram.'

Her closed eyelid opened, showing an empty black hole.

The boy turned pale and ran away.

'Moron,' the old lady sneered.

'We have to stay alert,' she panted into her mobile. 'Time for new action. The R.O.W. Club for ever.' The old lady peered left and right. 'I'm hanging up now. The walls have ears . . .'

10

Her!

Tim and Alfie didn't say a word to each other during dinner. Alfie was angry because Tim had been embarrassed about Dad. And he couldn't stop thinking about Noura and Luke.

Tim was angry because Alfie was angry.

Mum was staring into space and seemed miles away.

'It's very quiet here at the table,' Dad said. He was wearing his favourite tea cosy on his head: the elephant. 'Shall I play a song on my accordion? A bit of mood music?'

Nobody answered.

Suddenly Mum stood up. 'Now I remember. I forgot to buy a new broom. I need a really good one. And I have to go to my course.'

'Good idea,' Dad said. 'But shall I play a song first?'

'Well, that's really not necessary, dear,' Mum said.

But Dad had already turned round to the big case leaning against the wall behind him. He lifted out the Green Monster.

'There, time for a beautiful ballad,' he said, turning around.

All of the chairs were empty. There was no one left at the table.

'How odd,' Dad said. 'They must have gone to the toilet.'

Alfie went up to his bedroom, passing Tim on the landing, but they both turned their heads and didn't say a word. Tim went into his room and slammed the door behind him. Alfie did the same, slamming his door even harder. He flopped down on his bed. He couldn't be bothered getting undressed and he was too tired to look for his pyjamas. There was a brand-new duvet on his bed. And a soft new pillow too.

Dear old Mum, thought Alfie, but he wasn't able to be really happy. His stomach was hurting from the argument with Tim.

He sighed, laid his glasses on the bedside table and closed his eyes. He didn't want to think about the argument any more. And he didn't want to think about Luke either.

He fell asleep almost straightaway.

The light shining in through Alfie's bedroom window woke him up. He opened his sleepy eyes.

The moonbeams tickled his skin, as if he was lying under a fine shower. His muscles tingled and his blood rushed through his veins. He felt fur growing on his arms. His nose changed into a snout. And his fingers and toes grew claws.

It was werewolf time! Fantastic! He'd even

forgotten about the argument.

Alfie leapt out of bed in one smooth movement. He straightened his glasses. His pointy wolf's ears stood up.

'*Wrow.*'

He climbed out of the window and rolled off the roof, landing in the garden with a soft thud, then jumping up easily. He looked around. Everything was fine. No one had seen him. The houses were dark, the whole street was asleep and the full moon was smiling down on him.

'*Wrow.* Hello, moon,' Alfie growled.

The stars winked.

Alfie was almost out of the street when he noticed something strange and stopped. There was one house where the lights were still on.

Huh? he thought, his heart pounding. That's impossible. That house has been empty for ages. Nobody lives there any more. That used to be Mrs Chalker's house.

He hesitated for a moment, then crossed the road and slipped into the garden. It had

been a long time since anyone had done any gardening and tall weeds now stood where there had once been a chicken coop.

Alfie peered through the undergrowth at the window. There was someone there! A shadow was moving behind the glass.

Suddenly the curtain jerked aside. Alfie dropped to the ground quickly, behind a bush with red flowers.

Yellow light shone into the garden from inside the room, revealing a black silhouette. Alfie froze. The shadow was as skinny and scrawny as a scarecrow. With a thin hooked nose, a silly feather hat on its head and an umbrella in one hand.

'Oh no,' he groaned. 'It wasn't a dream after all. It's her! She's back!'

11

Warning

Mrs Chalker pushed the window open wide and Alfie heard a strange sound: *creak-crack, creak-crack . . .*

She's crunching like a bag of crisps, thought Alfie. She must have gone rusty in the RCUPA.

The woman stuck her head out of the window.

'Hello, dear moon,' she said in a sweet voice. 'You look as lovely as ever. As beautiful and full as a round of cheese.' She blew the moon a kiss.

Completely bonkers, thought Alfie. She's back and she's madder than ever! He crawled in under the bush when she looked in his direction.

His memories of Mrs Chalker were all bad. Sometimes he even had nightmares about her. Mrs Chalker hated werewolves. She'd already caught him once, in a vicious iron trap. Fortunately Grandpa Werewolf had saved him in the nick of time. Together with Tim and Mum and Dad.

Alfie had been very relieved when they locked Mrs Chalker up in the RCUPA. Permanently, he'd hoped. But now she was back and he didn't understand how it was possible.

Mrs Chalker's eyes gleamed in the moonlight as she looked around the garden. Her eyes were like searchlights sweeping left and right.

She can see me, thought Alfie. I'm sure of it. That witch looks straight through darkness. Next thing I know she'll be burning holes in my fur with those creepy eyes of hers.

He pressed his muzzle against the ground and froze.

'Ah, my beautiful garden,' Mrs Chalker whispered. 'I love all your little flowers and all your little blades of grass. I even love your naughty little weeds and thistles. Just look how wild you've grown. I've neglected you for far too long. Oh yes, I have! And it was all my own fault. I was a wicked woman. Bad, bad Chalker!'

She gave herself a slap on the cheek. *WHAP!*

'Ow! But I've changed, dear moon. Thanks to the loving care of the RCUPA.'

Alfie couldn't believe his ears. He didn't dare to look up, but what had happened to Mrs Chalker? There was a loud honking noise, like an elephant farting. Alfie pushed aside a leafy branch and peered at the window. Mrs Chalker was flapping a floral handkerchief. Tears ran down her cheeks and a gleaming thread of snot hung from her nose.

Yuck, thought Alfie. Moonlit Chalker juice.

Mrs Chalker looked back up at the moon. 'I have to protect the children,' she blubbered. 'All of them. Especially the werewolf children. I have to warn them, dear moon. They're in terrible danger.' Mrs Chalker sighed deeply. 'I'm afraid no one will believe me. They still hate me. And I can't blame them. But I must warn them! Otherwise horrible things will happen.' She peered around the garden again. *Creak-crack*. Then she banged the window shut. Alfie stayed where he was, motionless.

He wondered if it was a trap. Is she about to leap out with her umbrella?

The curtains were drawn. The light was off.

Alfie crawled over the ground and through the weeds, looking back over his shoulder the whole time, but the window stayed dark and Mrs Chalker was nowhere in sight. As if she had just been a ghost. Alfie stood up, totally confused.

'Did I hear right? Has Mrs Chalker suddenly turned good?' He shook his head. 'I have to go straight to Grandpa Werewolf.'

He tore off down the street.

12

Rowing Boat

It was quiet in Werewolf Wood. The full moon shone silently through the branches and the leaves swayed gently in the breeze.

Suddenly there was a rustling sound. Alfie was running under the tall trees, kicking up leaves.

'*Wrow*, Grandpa, where are you?'

No answer came, but Alfie heard something else. Voices. A song he knew.

'*Rub, rub, rub away,*
If they cry or shout,

Rubbedy, rubbedy, rubbedy, rubbedy,
Rub the last one out.'

Without stopping to think, Alfie dived behind a bush. That song again, he thought, peering through the leaves.

The singing grew louder. Thin shadows moved in the moonlight. They were coming down the path and singing with grating voices.

For a second Alfie's heart stopped. It

looked like Mrs Chalker. And he was seeing double. What was going on? He rubbed his eyes, but there really were two of her. And they were carrying a rowing boat on their shoulders.

Wow, those old ladies are super strong, thought Alfie. What are they doing carrying a rowing boat around Werewolf Wood this late at night?

The two ladies came closer. Alfie held his breath. Checked slippers shuffled past the bush he was hiding behind.

'Rub them out!' screeched one of the women.

'Kill them dead,' yelled the other.

'Make an ashtray from the head,' they sang together.

Then they both giggled very loudly.

Alfie stayed where he was and didn't move. He held his breath and squeezed his eyes shut while the singing slowly disappeared into the distance. What did it all mean?

13

Old Dears

Tim had never had an argument with Alfie before and now he tossed and turned under his duvet. Lying on his left. Right. Stomach. Back. His nose itched. He had cramp in his leg.

Finally he couldn't stand it any more. He slipped out of bed, pulled on his slippers, walked to Alfie's room and knocked quietly on the door.

'Alfie, can I come in?'

No answer. Gently, Tim pushed open the door, revealing an empty bed and an open window. The full moon cast a big spot of light on the floor. Tim slapped himself on the forehead.

'Of course, it's full moon. I put the cross on the calendar myself. I forgot all about it! Alfie is outside somewhere as a werewolf.' Tim shuffled downstairs sadly, wishing Alfie was home. I need to make it up with him, he thought, otherwise I'll never get back to sleep. He's my best friend, my adopted brother.

Downstairs in the hall, he heard the sound of a waterfall. 'Alfie, is that you?'

The toilet door opened and Dad emerged.

'Ooph,' said Tim, pinching his nose shut.

Dad grimaced. 'Sorry, I shouldn't have finished off those beans.' He was wearing a wetsuit and a diving mask. Mum and Dad had recently bought a waterbed and normal pyjamas just didn't seem right to him any more. Instead of slippers he was wearing flippers.

He stared at Tim with surprise. 'What are

you doing up this late anyway?'

Tim hesitated.

'I couldn't sleep.'

'Why's that?'

Tim looked down at his feet. 'I had a fight with Alfie and, um . . .' He fell silent.

Dad scratched behind his ear thoughtfully. 'I understand. If you've had a fight, it's hard to sleep.'

Tim nodded.

'What did you argue about?'

Tim kept his eyes on his feet and shrugged. He didn't dare say.

'A-ha, you can't tell me,' Dad said. 'Where's Alfie now?'

'I'm not sure,' Tim said. 'Maybe Werewolf Wood.'

Suddenly they heard noise from outside. Voices.

'What's that?' Dad said. 'Is that Alfie?'

Tim ran to the front door. Dad slid the mask down over his eyes.

'Wait, Tim, I'll come with you,' he called, following Tim in his flippers. He looked like a penguin wearing a diving mask.

The moment the front door opened, the voices were clearer.

> 'Rub, rub, rub-a-dub.
> Rub them out in waves . . .'

Astonished, Tim and Dad walked into the garden. Standing in the road next to a parked car were two skinny figures. Little old ladies with a rowing boat on top of their car. With grating voices, they sang their strange song.

'Rubbedy, rubbedy, rubbedy, rubbedy,
Till they're in their graves.'

The crones looked at each other and cackled with laughter.

'What are those old dears doing out on the street so late at night?' Dad asked. 'And why is their singing so loud and horrible? They should take me and my accordion as an example.'

The ladies suddenly stopped singing and jerked their heads round. The moonlight gleamed yellow in their eyes as they hunched their shoulders and curled their fingers like claws. Slowly they began to shuffle silently towards Dad and Tim . . .

14

Where is everyone?

Alfie emerged from behind the bush. The women were gone. They'd marched out of the forest with the rowing boat on their shoulders. Alfie had heard the sound of a car and then he'd waited behind the bush for another ten minutes just to be on the safe side. I have to get to Grandpa Werewolf's fast, he thought.

Grandpa lived in a brand-new treehouse that Leo had built for him. It was a fantastic home with a super-deluxe lift made of planks and ropes. Green patches painted on the outside made it almost invisible between the leaves and the branches. There was even room for the Scoffle, Grandpa's mysterious pet.

Alfie dug his claws into the bark, climbed up quickly and knocked on the door.

No answer and no snoring either. Grandpa Werewolf probably wasn't home. And the Scoffle was probably asleep too, in a corner somewhere or under Grandpa's bed.

I'll see if Leo is around, thought Alfie, lowering himself down from the tree and running back into the wood.

'Leo! Where are you? Wake up, sleepyhead. Leeeee-ohhhhh!' He stopped for a moment to howl at the moon. *'Wrow-awooooo woohoo!'* The ancient cry of the werewolf.

Alfie listened. Nothing! Strange. Where are they? he thought. Where's Grandpa Werewolf? Where's Leo? And what about Noura? Why isn't she here?

Suddenly a horrible thought rose up in him. Maybe she went to see that stupid Luke . . . He shook his head. *Wrow,* don't think such stupid things, Alfie.

He ran on, climbing high in trees to peer through branches, sliding down – *swish-swish* – and running on even further. He poked his nose into hollow trees and peered into birds' nests and badgers' dens. Again Alfie howled at the moon.

It stayed quiet in Werewolf Wood. No werewolves answered.

Finally Alfie gave up and shuffled along the path sadly.

'Wrow! What's going on? Where is everyone?'

Suddenly something shot out from a bush and grabbed him by the ankle . . .

15

Rowing

'Good evening, ladies,' Dad said cheerfully.

The old women didn't say a word, they just shuffled closer. The two of them looked awfully alike: hooked noses, long chins and funny-looking cardigans. One of them only had one eye. The other had just one ear. They slunk around Tim and Dad like two battle-scarred tomcats. Dad looked at Tim and shrugged.

'It's the middle of the night, ladies,' he said. 'Aren't you afraid to be out so late?'

The oldies exchanged a glance then

burst out laughing.

'Afraid?' said the lady with one eye.

'Us?' said the other one. 'We're not afraid of anything.'

'Not werewolves, not vampires, not ghosts.'

The woman with one ear pointed at Dad. 'And we're definitely not afraid of funny little men like you. Nothing scares us.'

They exchanged another glance.

'Well, almost nothing, sister. Nothing except creepy monsters.'

'True enough, you old bag; nothing except extremely creepy monsters.'

Again they started to laugh at the top of their voices.

'But lucky for us we never bump into any of them. Mostly just werewolves.'

The old women suddenly peered at Tim. They pinched his cheek and sniffed his neck. One pulled his ear. The other one buried her nose in his hair and took a deep breath.

'Hey,' Tim said, stepping back. 'Get off!'

'Ladies, stop that!' Dad said forcefully. He

stood in front of Tim and held out his arms. His diving mask misted over with anger.

'Would you please stop pinching my son? And don't sniff him! That's, um . . . nasal harassment. Otherwise I'll . . . I'll hit you, I will. Or else I'll call the police or something!'

The two old ladies glared at him.

'Hey, don't I know you from somewhere?' Dad said, quickly wiping his mask clean. 'Weren't you at my performance on the street corner this afternoon?'

The two women burst into cackling laughter. Their eyes gleamed with a dingy, yellowish glow.

'What are you doing out so late anyway?' Dad asked. 'Old girls like you should be tucked up in bed by now. With your false teeth in a glass on the bedside table and snoring away with a hot-water bottle on your stomach.'

The ladies stared at him.

'Rowing,' snapped one of them, pointing at the boat on the roof of their car. 'We go rowing together. And we were just out for a nice row in the woods. Does that satisfy your curiosity, frogman?'

The old ladies giggled.

'Dad, these grannies are barmy!' Tim whispered. 'I think they're creepy. They look like Mrs Chalker and that's twice as creepy. Do you think there's a Chalker Club?'

Dad stared into space dreamily. 'Relax, son. It's nothing to worry about. Rowing at full moon is an unusual sport. It's very . . . um . . . different. I wouldn't mind trying it sometime myself.'

'Ouch!' Tim cried.

The old lady with one eye had sneaked past Dad to jab Tim with a silver needle. Her one eye leered curiously at the blood dripping from his thumb.

'That hurt, you old bat!' Tim screamed. 'Are you mad or what?'

'Hmm, no werewolf reaction,' the old lady mumbled. 'He's not one of them.'

The old ladies leant towards each other and started whispering. Suddenly Tim saw the letters on the backs of their cardigans: R.O.W. Club.

'Dad, look,' he said. 'They're—'

Just then a door opened down the street. Someone hurried down a garden path. Someone in a feather hat, who waved an umbrella angrily as she approached. *Creak-crack, creak-crack . . .*

Tim froze. 'Another Mrs Chalker!'

Even Dad's face turned pale. 'As if it wasn't bad enough already. Now there's three of them . . .'

16

What's going on?

WHAM! Alfie fell over on his snout.
Something was still holding tight to his
ankle. A loud yawn emerged from the bush.

'Owaaaa!'

Leaves rustled, branches snapped.

A hat popped out of the bush. It was on
top of a black wolf's head.

'*Wrow*, Grandpa Werewolf! What are you
doing in that bush?'

Grandpa Werewolf let go of Alfie's ankle.
He gave a shy grin, stood up and wrestled
his way out of the shrubbery. His raincoat

was crumpled and his hat was dented.

'Ooph, sorry, Alfie. Nice to see you. I was looking for your cousin Leo. And then I, um . . . fell asleep. In that bush. Things like that happen at my age.' Grandpa Werewolf reached into the bush and pulled out a walking stick. 'Sorry about grabbing you. I was dreaming that I was young again and I, um . . . I was chasing Grandma Werewolf. You understand?' A big grin appeared on his face at the memory. 'I almost had her.'

Alfie looked at him in surprise. It was the first time he'd ever heard him mention Grandma Werewolf.

Grandpa Werewolf saw Alfie's questioning look. 'Oh, I'll tell you about her one day,' he mumbled.

Alfie nodded. '*Wrow*. I'm glad I found you, Grandpa. I was starting to get worried. It's full moon but Werewolf Wood's deserted. I called and called, but no werewolves answered. Not Leo, not Noura and not you either. Then I suddenly saw two old ladies with a rowing boat. They looked like Mrs

Chalker. I thought I was seeing double.'

Grandpa Werewolf leant silently on his walking stick. His pupils gleamed a dark black. The grin was gone from his face.

'They looked like Chalker? What's going on? Chalker's still locked up, isn't she?'

'Not any more, Grandpa. She's back.' Quickly Alfie told him what he'd seen in Mrs Chalker's garden. Grandpa listened carefully, then shook his head and let out a deep sigh.

'What a strange story. Has Chalker turned over a new leaf all of a sudden?' He narrowed his eyes to slits and peered thoughtfully at Alfie. 'Old ladies with a rowing boat, you say? That is very strange too.'

'*Wrow*, what do you mean, Grandpa?'

Grandpa raised his walking stick and pointed at the trees. 'Do you see any water here, Alfie? Why are those old ladies carrying a rowing boat around with them? There aren't any lakes in Werewolf Wood. There's nowhere to row. And why do they look like Chalker?' Grandpa rubbed his snout. 'I'm

worried about Leo all of a sudden. Where's
he been all evening? He's disappeared . . .'

17

A Smile

'Choker, Cheeker, come here. What are you doing?' Mrs Chalker rushed past Dad and Tim. She pointed at the lady with one eye. 'Choker, what have I told you?'

Then she looked at the one who was missing an ear. 'That goes for you too, Cheeker. You don't listen!'

Suddenly she raised her umbrella and – WHACK! WHACK! – brought it down on the elderly ladies' heads.

'Get that boat off the car and go inside. And don't you ever bother these nice people again.'

Choker and Cheeker glared at Chalker. Cheeker gave her the 'V' sign and Choker stuck out her tongue. Mrs Chalker gritted her teeth. Then she moved like lightning and grabbed Choker by the tongue. 'You want to lose this too, do you? No? Well, behave yourself then.' She jabbed Cheeker's foot with her umbrella. 'You too. Get to work. Don't make me lose my temper . . .'

The two ladies screamed.

'Grab that boat and go inside,' Mrs Chalker screeched. 'Otherwise you'll be sorry. Move it!'

Cursing and grumbling, the old ladies walked over to the car and yanked the rowing boat off the roof. Dad rushed over.

'Shall I help carry it, ladies?'

He grabbed the rowing boat with two hands. 'Huh, that's funny, there's a lid on this boat. It looks like a coffin. What's it got a lid for?'

'To keep out the rain, you halfwit,' Choker shouted.

'Let go, moron,' Cheeker yelled.

Choker gave Dad a dirty look. 'Get lost!'

'OK, OK,' Dad said, quickly stepping aside. 'I was just offering.'

Mrs Chalker shook her umbrella at her sisters. 'Choker, Cheeker, go and wash your mouths out this instant! I don't want to ever hear you being rude to these people again!'

Grumbling under their breath, the two of them lugged the rowing boat up the garden path.

Pretty impressive all the same, thought Tim. A boat like that must be heavy. Those ladies have muscles of iron.

'There,' Mrs Chalker said, turning back to Tim and Dad after the women had gone into the house. 'I'm dreadfully sorry, dear neighbours. I'm so ashamed of my sisters. We're triplets, but I'm afraid they are both extremely coarse and not respectable at all.' Mrs Chalker gave a cautious smile. Her jaw creaked softly. 'I'm trying to turn them into good girls, but I'm not making much progress.'

Tim and Dad gaped at the smile on Mrs Chalker's face. It was like a miracle. The old Mrs Chalker never smiled. She was always angry, with her mouth set in a scowl that looked like it had been painted on. Now she was grinning from ear to ear. And her bones creaked with every move she made.

That's almost just as creepy, thought Tim.

Dad coughed and raised his diving mask to his forehead. 'Hmm, Mrs Chalker. What a surprise to see you here. I thought you were at the RCUPA. You never used to be so . . . I mean, you were rather . . . How can I put it?'

For a moment, the smile on Mrs Chalker's face tightened.

Uh-oh, Tim thought. Dad shouldn't have said that . . .

18

An Angel

The smile slowly returned to Mrs Chalker's face. 'Yes, that is true. Feel free to say it out loud, neighbour. I was a wicked person. I was bad, bad Chalker.'

Tears shone in the corners of Mrs Chalker's eyes. She sniffed as her nose began to run.

Dad glanced at Tim and shrugged. 'Come now. You mustn't exaggerate. It's not as if you were so terribly evil.'

Still blubbering, Mrs Chalker nodded. 'I was worse! Even my own sisters were scared to death of me. When we were young I told them stories about a gruesome monster. A horrific, blood-drinking, bone-crunching cupboard monster. Even now they sometimes wake up screaming. The poor fools think the monster is still searching for them.' Mrs Chalker shook her head sadly. 'Yes, I was a nasty piece of work. But that's all in the past. I'm cured, thanks to the care of the RCUPA. They let me go, the sweethearts. I stand here before you a completely different person. Nice flippers, by the way.'

Dad blushed and bowed slightly. 'Wow, my compliments, Mrs Chalker. That's brilliant of you to have made such a complete recovery.'

Mrs Chalker nodded. *Crack,* went her neck.

'I'm very pleased about it too, neighbour. I now dedicate myself to good deeds. I have a workshop behind my house where I collect clothing for poor children from underprivileged families.'

'Charity work,' Dad said. 'That too!'

Mrs Chalker nodded again. 'We make old clothes as good as new. Choker and Cheeker help me. They're good with needles and knives and things like that. They love anything sharp.'

Tim swallowed. 'Really, Mrs Chalker?'

She patted him on the head and gently pinched his cheek. A shiver ran down his spine.

'It really is true, little boy. But now I have to go and make sure those two don't set fire to the house.' She turned around and walked back to her front door.

Tim and Dad looked at each other in astonishment.

'That was . . .' Dad began.

'Very strange,' Tim continued.

Dad nodded. 'I don't really know what to make of it.'

'Maybe a miracle happened,' Tim suggested.

'Yes,' Dad said. 'That woman has changed

completely. First she was a witch and now she's an angel.'

'A creaking angel,' Tim said. 'And a triplet. I still don't altogether trust her . . .'

19

Blue Day

Alfie stretched. It was morning again and he was back in his own bed. The sun shone through the curtains and he immediately remembered the previous evening. Kind Mrs Chalker, the old ladies with the rowing boat and Grandpa Werewolf.

Leo and Noura hadn't shown up and when morning came Alfie had gone back home and crept into bed, where he'd changed into a boy again. Without claws and without werewolf fur. Just Alfie Span with normal boy's teeth.

Now he had to get up. It was time for school.

Mum and Dad were sitting at the breakfast table. Mum had curlers in her hair and Dad had dyed his hair blue.

'I'm having a blue day today,' he said. 'I think I'll sing a new blue song. Get it? The blues!' Immediately he burst into song.

> 'I woke up this morning,
> It was extremely cold,
> I felt so down and lonely,
> I felt I was so old,
> I wanted to get going,
> So I looked round for my shoes,
> But they weren't in the cupboard,
> And then I got the blues,
> The lost shoes blues.'

Alfie was still half asleep and just nodded. He wasn't in the mood for music. Especially not Dad's weird songs.

'Where's Tim?'

'He's already gone to school,' Mum said, pouring Alfie a cup of tea. 'We let you sleep in an extra hour. Because of last night's full moon.'

Dad winked. 'I wrote a note for Mr French. Telling him you had to go to the dentist's, Dr Drillhard-Sweetpea.'

Alfie burst out laughing. 'Dr Drillhard-Sweetpea? There aren't any dentists called Drillhard-Sweetpea.'

Dad grinned and shrugged. 'I had to make up something. Mr French is hardly going to believe that you turned into a werewolf last night and didn't get enough sleep. Here, eat some toast and cheese. You didn't devour any chickens last night, I hope.'

'What? No, thank goodness.'

Suddenly Mum jumped up. 'Oh, bother!'

'What is it, dear?' Dad asked. 'Did *you* devour a chicken?'

Mum giggled. 'No, silly, of course not. I forgot to buy a new broom again. I need a very good one.'

'Is it really necessary?' Dad asked.

Mum nodded. 'Yep. I even dreamt about it. I have to buy a very good, new broom. And it's almost time I left for my course.' Then she walked out of the kitchen.

Dad looked at Alfie and winked. 'A broom that appears in your dreams? That must be a scary housewife secret.'

Alfie laughed. 'Probably, Dad. What kind of course is Mum doing?

'Um . . .' Dad racked his brains. 'I think she said room lighting.'

'Oh, nice,' said Alfie.

A little later Alfie left for school.

It's too bad Tim's already gone, he thought, walking out of the garden. We still haven't made up and I really want to. I—

Surprised, he froze on the spot. A strange vehicle was approaching on the pavement. A clothes rack on wheels with small trousers, coats, jumpers and overalls swinging back and forth. The rack looked like it was full of dancing toddlers . . . And it was racing straight at him.

From behind the rack he heard loud puffs and sighs.

Alfie jumped out of the way just in time, toppling backwards on to a low hedge.

'Blerk!' With a look of disgust, he spat out a few small leaves.

'Oh, I'm so sorry, dear boy,' a voice said. 'I didn't do it on purpose, you know.'

Alfie looked up with fright. It was a voice he knew very well.

Standing behind the racing rack was Mrs Chalker. She looked startled. Even her feather hat was crooked.

'Here, let me give you a hand,' she said, bending over towards him.

Alfie shook his head. The last thing he wanted was to touch Mrs Chalker. Quickly he got back up on to his feet. Mrs Chalker looked at him anxiously.

'Are you all right, son? It's all my fault. I wasn't paying attention.' She sighed and wiped the sweat from her forehead. 'I just picked up a new rack of clothes for poor, deprived children. I'm taking it to my workshop. But I should have been more careful. You're not angry at me, are you?'

Alfie looked down at the ground and shook his head.

Mrs Chalker sighed with relief. 'Thank goodness. I'm glad to hear it. You're such a

sweet boy. I'll get back to work then. I want to cheer up a few poor children with these clothes this very day. Bye-bye, son, I'll see you later, because I have a surprise for you.' Then she rolled the rack up her own garden path. *Creak-crack-creak . . .*

Alfie hadn't said a word. His mouth was hanging open. He couldn't believe what had happened. Chalker had run him down, but not on purpose, apparently. She really did seem to have changed into a kind-hearted little old lady.

Could it be true? thought Alfie, scratching his head. What does she mean? How come she's going to see me later? And what kind of surprise does she have for me?

20

The Moon

'Where were you last night, Noura?' Alfie whispered. 'I was waiting for you in Werewolf Wood.'

Mr French drew a yellow circle on the blackboard. 'Look, this is the moon,' he said. 'Yesterday was full moon. At full moon, the moon is completely round. The moon has a big influence on the Earth.'

Noura looked at Alfie. 'Sorry, Alfie. There was a party at our house. There were aunts and uncles and lots of cousins. Everyone stayed until really late, so I couldn't get out.'

She ran her fingers through her curls. 'My parents still don't know I'm a werewolf. I had to hide in my room. In bed, under the blankets.'

Alfie nodded. 'You'll have to tell them one day.'

'I know,' Noura whispered. 'I was bored out of my skull. It was full moon outside and I was inside lying under a blanket in my werewolf skin. Fortunately Luke called me on my mobile.'

Alfie sat up straight. 'Luke called you? At full moon? What for?' He glared at Luke, who was sitting a few desks away. Luke smiled, but Alfie didn't smile back.

Where did Luke get the nerve to call Noura? The idiot with his smooth face and his trendy collar.

'Don't make a fuss, Alfie,' Noura whispered. 'He just wanted to ask me something about the homework. We got talking. About things. This and that. He only moved here recently and he still doesn't know anyone. It was nice. We talked for an hour.'

Alfie stared at her in disbelief. 'An hour? How could you talk to him that long, Noura? Your voice changes too when you're a werewolf. He must have noticed.'

'Don't be silly. He just said, "You sound a bit growly all of a sudden."'

Alfie groaned. 'See! And what did you say?'

Noura pointed to her throat. 'Sore throat, losing my voice.'

Alfie sighed. 'You think he believed you? You sound normal again today. You got your voice back in a hurry. That must seem pretty suspicious.'

Noura started to lose her patience. 'Of course he believed me! Don't be so jealous, Alfie.'

'Jealous? I—'

'Alfie and Noura, pay attention!' Mr French said. 'Today we're talking about the moon. The moon has a great influence on the rise and fall of seawater. The tides, in other words. Who knows something else

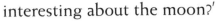

interesting about the moon?'

Luke put up his finger immediately. 'Werewolves.'

Both Alfie and Noura spun around. Luke smiled.

'What do you mean, Luke?' Mr French asked.

'What do you think I mean?' Luke answered. 'Some people change into werewolves at full moon. There are books about it.'

'Really? How interesting,' Mr French said. 'What happens to them?'

'Duh!' Luke said. 'Everyone knows that! Those dudes grow claws and a fur coat. And then they start to growl.'

Alfie burst into a spontaneous coughing fit. Noura choked and turned bright red. Just then the door of the classroom opened. *Creak-crack, creak-crack* . . .

'Good morning, dear children.' There was someone standing in the doorway. Feather hat. Umbrella . . .

21

Party Time!

'Surprise!'

All eyes turned to the door.

'Oh, no,' Alfie groaned.

Noura looked at him in surprise. 'Do you know her?'

'It's Mrs Chalker,' Alfie whispered. 'You know, the lady up the street, the one who—'

The next instant Mrs Chalker was stepping into the classroom. *Creak-crack.*

'She creaks like an old bed,' Ahmed whispered, next to Luke.

Mrs Chalker moved over to stand in front of the blackboard. 'Good morning, children. Here I am with a nice surprise.' She stood there with her umbrella and hat, holding a big white box in her hands. 'Just look what I've got here.'

Mr French walked over to her. He moved close and put his mouth up to her ear. Then he said clearly and very loudly, 'MADAM, YOU'RE AT THE WRONG PLACE. THIS ISN'T THE OLD PEOPLE'S HOME, IT'S A PRIMARY SCHOOL.'

Mrs Chalker giggled. 'Relax, teacher-boy. I may creak, but I'm not deaf. I'm here with good news.' She looked around the class cheerfully and acted as if Mr French wasn't even there. Alfie tried to hide behind his hands.

'Hello, dear boy,' Mrs Chalker said. 'What a delightful class you have. All little darlings.'

Everyone looked at Alfie.

'Hey, Alfie, is that your grandma?' Luke grinned.

Alfie blushed bright red and slipped down as far as he could behind his desk. Mrs Chalker tapped the blackboard with her umbrella.

'Boys and girls, I have an important question. Whose birthday is it today?'

The children looked at each other.

'No one's,' Ahmed shouted. 'No parties in the class today.'

Then someone stuck up his finger. Luke.

'Mine,' he said. 'It's my birthday today.'

Mr French looked at Luke with surprise. 'Really, Luke? I didn't even know. How strange.'

Mrs Chalker smiled. 'See? How fortunate that I've come here today. You *do* have something to celebrate.'

Ahmed threw his hands up. 'Hooray, party time!'

Everyone cheered. Everyone except Alfie.

'Happy birthday, Luke,' Noura whispered.

Alfie scowled. 'Humph. His birthday.

So what? Everyone has a birthday. As if there's anything special about that. If it's even true . . .'

Mrs Chalker walked over to Luke, put the box down on his desk carefully and flapped open the lid. 'Look what I have here.'

Luke looked in the box. 'Strawberry cake,' he called out. 'An enormous strawberry cake with a thick layer of whipped cream.'

Mrs Chalker smiled. 'A delicious strawberry cake for the whole class. Thanks to you, little boy.'

Alfie saw her wink at Luke. What's she doing that for? he wondered.

'It's your birthday, so you get to say,' Mrs Chalker said.

Luke looked up at her with a frown. 'Say what?'

Mrs Chalker chuckled secretively. 'Who you'd like to give the first piece of cake to.'

Luke didn't hesitate, but pointed straight at Noura. 'Her!'

22

Lucky Girl

All heads turned towards Noura, who blushed. Alfie felt a terrible urge to bite Luke as hard as he could. Too bad I'm not a werewolf in the daytime, he thought.

'Ah,' Mrs Chalker said. 'So that girl is the lucky one. Lovely. Just lovely.'

For a second Alfie thought he saw her wink at Luke again. He even thought Luke was winking back. You see, he thought, they're in it together. Chalker is helping Luke take Noura away from me. Then he shook his head. Stop it, stop it, I'm thinking crazy things.

Mrs Chalker walked over with the cake box and studied Noura carefully. 'So, little girl, you're the one! What's your name?'

What's she getting at? thought Alfie.

'Noura,' answered Noura.

'Noura, you're in luck. If you ask me, the birthday boy has his eye on you.'

Noura turned even redder than the strawberries. Under his breath, Alfie let out a growl of misery. Mrs Chalker pulled a big knife out from under her coat.

'Ahhhh,' the children gasped in fright.

Mrs Chalker sniggered and looked around the class, then cut a big piece of cake and put it down in front of Noura on a paper plate.

'See, dear, I've thought of everything.'

Noura smiled shyly.

'Just a moment,' Mrs Chalker said. 'You mustn't eat cake with your fingers. That's why I've brought pretty little silver cake forks for everyone. Very stylish. Here, the first one is for you.'

She held the fork out to Noura.

Noura looked at it. Her face turned white and she didn't take the fork.

Alfie saw her hands shaking and immediately understood what was going on. Noura can't bear silver, he thought. Just like me, because she's a werewolf too. We werewolves are allergic to silver. It can even be fatal.

'Come now, Noura,' Mrs Chalker said in a friendly voice. 'Don't be shy. Take a bite. It's scrumptious strawberry cake.' She speared a piece with the fork. 'Here, look how yummy it is. Come on, open wide . . . Take a bite!'

'Bite, bite, bite!' chanted the class.

Slowly Mrs Chalker brought the fork closer to Noura's mouth. Noura moved her head back. She looked pale. There were drops of sweat on her forehead. She had even gone a bit cross-eyed. She looked like she was about to faint.

'Noura, are you OK?' Mr French asked.

Alfie leapt up.

'Stop!' he shouted, pointing at the cake
fork. 'Please put that thing away, Mrs
Chalker. Noura's allergic.'

Mrs Chalker looked at him in surprise.

'Oh, really? Is she? What's this sweet little
girl allergic to?'

Alfie swallowed.

Mrs Chalker winked and bent over him. 'I
know what you're allergic to, dear boy,' she
whispered. 'Silver, of course. Don't you

worry about that. That's our little secret. But what's the story with this girl?'

'Um . . .' Alfie said.

Just then Luke stood up. 'I know . . .'

23

Cake!

'Really. I know,' Luke said again.

Alfie gaped at Luke. How did he—

'Noura is allergic to . . . strawberries!'

Mrs Chalker looked at Luke with big eyes. 'Strawberries? Really?'

Noura nodded her head furiously.

Mrs Chalker coughed. 'Oh, you dear! And I was trying to give you strawberry cake. How stupid of me. I should hang my head in shame. The others will just have to eat up the whole cake.' She cut the cake into pieces and laid the silver cake forks next to them.

'Sorry, boys and girls. It was lovely to visit, but I must be going. Enjoy the cake.'

In the doorway she stopped suddenly and turned around. 'Oh, before I forget, children. If you happen to bump into two ladies that look like me . . .' Mrs Chalker looked at them with a serious expression on her face. 'Just keep walking! They're called Cheeker and Choker, and they're very dangerous.' Within a second she was gone. The creaking of her bones faded away down the corridor.

The children were silent for a moment, and then they all roared, 'Cake!'

The strawberry cake was almost finished. Even Mr French had eaten a large piece. His chin was covered with red smudges.

'I don't know who that creaky old lady was,' he said. 'She was a strange woman, but a very kind one. She was an angel and she brought us a delicious cake.'

Alfie and Noura were the only ones who hadn't had any cake. Luke stuffed the last piece into his mouth with his hand. The silver cake fork was lying on his desk.

'I never use those snooty little forks,' he said, with one eye leering at Alfie. 'So you're allergic too, are you? Just like Noura?'

Alfie nodded. Except I'm allergic to you, you smart alec, he thought.

Then the bell rang.

'Are you coming to Werewolf Wood tonight?' Alfie asked Noura as they walked through the school gates.

Noura nodded.

'Phew,' she said. 'That was close. That silver fork made me feel really sick. Lucky for me Luke saved me just in time. He really thought I was allergic to strawberries.'

'Yeah, yeah,' Alfie said. 'I saved you too, you know. I was the one who told Chalker that you were allergic in the first place.'

They heard footsteps behind them.

'Noura, wait a sec.'

They looked back. It was Luke. He stopped and stood there panting.

Humph, thought Alfie, he pants like a dog. And those eyes are just as doggy.

Luke smiled at Noura. 'I'm throwing a party tonight. Would you like to come?'

Alfie sniggered quietly. Tough luck, Lukey, he thought. Of course Noura doesn't want to go to your stupid party.

'Oh, how nice,' Noura said. 'I'd love to.'

Alfie's mouth dropped.

Luke nodded. 'Great. It starts at eight o'clock. And, um, no strawberry cake. I promise.' Luke looked at Alfie. 'Sorry, Alfie, there's no room for you. Our house is full. Bye.' He handed a note to Noura and left.

Alfie could hardly believe it. 'Noura, you can't go to Luke's tonight. It's still full moon. We were going—'

'Don't worry, Alfie. Of course I'm going to Werewolf Wood.'

Alfie sighed. 'Phew.'

'After I've been to Luke's party,' Noura continued.

'Oh.'

Noura laughed. 'I'm not going to stay

there until I'm a werewolf, you know. I'll be gone long before then.'

Alfie walked on, grumbling. 'I still don't think it's a good idea.'

He walked into his street. In the distance two figures climbed out of a car with a rowing boat on the roof. Alfie recognized them at once.

'Cheeker and Choker,' he mumbled. 'That's what Mrs Chalker called them.'

The two women muttered to themselves, swearing and cursing.

'Grab that thing now, you miserable biddy.'

'No, you, you old bag.'

Alfie immediately hid behind a hedge. The women pulled a big black cauldron out of the car.

What's happening now? thought Alfie. What are those old ladies doing with a witch's cauldron? And why is the rowing boat on their car?

Still cursing, Cheeker and Choker dragged

the cauldron into the garden. Suddenly there was a sound coming from behind him: *creak-crack, creak-crack* . . .

'Hmmm, that's not polite, dear boy. It's bad manners to spy on people . . .'

25

The Cauldron

Alfie's shoulders tensed up. He was still scared of Mrs Chalker and now he felt her eyes pricking in the back of his neck. Slowly he turned around. Mrs Chalker smiled at him.

'Just kidding, son. If you ask me you're a little bit scared of my sisters. I understand that perfectly. They're vicious.'

Alfie nodded cautiously. Behind him he heard a door slam. Cheeker and Choker had gone inside.

'I, um, I'd rather stay away from them,

Mrs Chalker. They threw eggs at our front door.'

Mrs Chalker's eyes took on a fierce glow. 'What? I didn't know that. Your father didn't tell me. What a waste of eggs.' She gave a very loud sniff. 'Hmm, they deserve to be punished for that. Just you wait. Tonight I'll send them to bed without any supper. Or else I'll make them sleep in the cauldron as punishment, hee-hee.'

'The cauldron?' Alfie said. 'Is that for scary potions or something?'

Mrs Chalker giggled. 'Scary potions? Dear boy, of course not. They had to go and pick that cauldron up for me. I'm going to use it to boil up the second-hand clothes. They're often old and musty. Full of dirty fleas and moths and all kinds of bugs. But I only ever give spotless garments to poor, underprivileged children.' Mrs Chalker ran a long fingernail over Alfie's head. A shiver ran down his back.

'Hurry on home now, dear. My troublesome sisters are inside.'

Alfie ran off.

'Oh, son . . .' Mrs Chalker called after him. With a pounding heart, Alfie stopped. He didn't look back.

'Those two will get their punishment this evening. Tell your father, will you?'

Alfie ran into the living room. Dad was standing there with his accordion. Mum was walking through the room with a serving dish. Alfie put down his backpack.

'Guess who I bumped into three times today . . .' Then he fell silent.

Someone was sitting on the sofa in a raincoat. Hat on. Walking stick.

Grandpa Werewolf never visited in the daytime. Only when something serious was going on.

Leaning on his walking stick with his front paws, Grandpa slowly looked up at Alfie.

25

The Werewolf Blues

'Grandpa Werewolf! What are you doing here?' Alfie looked at his parents. Dad shrugged.

'It's Leo,' Grandpa said. 'He's— Oh, thank you.'

Mum put a plate of juicy steak down in front of Grandpa. 'Have something to eat first, Grandpa.'

Grandpa Werewolf nodded approvingly. 'Mmm, raw. Nice and bloody.' He took a big bite out of the steak and red juices ran down over his fangs. 'Delicious,' he growled.

'Grandma Werewolf used to serve them up like this in the old days.'

'Grandma Werewolf?' Dad asked.

'Grandpa will tell us about that another time,' Alfie said. 'We're talking about Leo now.'

Grandpa was staring into space with a dreamy expression. Alfie sat down next to him on the sofa.

'Grandpa, tell us. What's happened to Leo?'

Grandpa took off his hat. His eyes grew big.

'Leo hasn't come back, Alfie. There's no sign of him. He's been missing since yesterday. That's why I've come. To ask if he's been here.'

'No, we haven't seen him at all.'

Grandpa Werewolf sighed and scratched his black head. 'I thought as much, son. I'm very worried. Especially with those sisters hanging round.' He stared at his walking stick gloomily. 'I hope nothing bad has happened to him. Leo doesn't always look before he leaps. Sometimes he doesn't even look after he's landed.'

Dad hurried over to the sofa with his accordion. 'You're just a bit down, Grandpa. I think you've got the werewolf blues. Shall I play a song for you? To cheer you up? What about a nice werewolf tearjerker?'

'Preferably not,' Grandpa Werewolf growled, but Dad had already stretched out the accordion. A sigh like a moaning whale reverberated through the room. In the kitchen a glass bowl vibrated off the counter, smashing on the floor.

Dad started to sing.

> 'Oh, Leo went out walking,
> And never did return.
> He wasn't used to talking,
> Some words he'd never learn.
> And no one ever saw him . . .'

'No, no,' Mum and Alfie shouted together. 'Stop.'

Grandpa Werewolf had slid down off the

sofa with his ears drooping. He stared up at
Dad and his accordion in disbelief. Dad gave
a big toothy grin.

'Beautiful, isn't it, Grandpa? It knocked
you right off your feet.'

Grandpa hauled himself back up with
Alfie's help. Quickly he put his hat back on.

'I'm sorry, I have to get going.'

'Don't you want another bite of steak?'
Mum asked.

'And another song?' Dad asked.

Grandpa's eyes flashed from the
bloody steak to Dad's accordion. He shook
his head.

'My mouth's watering, but I have very
sensitive ears. Plus I need to feed the Scoffle.'

He hurried out of the door.

Dad smiled at Mum. 'He liked it. He must have. Did you see the tears in his eyes? And he was so moved his ears went floppy. Yet another fan.' Dad sighed. 'If it goes on like this I'll be really famous.'

Mum rolled her eyes. 'Definitely, dear.'

Alfie ran out of the door after Grandpa Werewolf. 'Wait a sec, Grandpa, I'll walk with you a little bit.'

26

Wrong

Alfie walked down the garden path next to Grandpa Werewolf, who was still a bit wobbly. Grandpa picked at one ear with a claw.

'Ooph, I think I've got a bit of that, um . . . song stuck in my ear. That accordion thing makes a terrible racket. You could use it to drive out witches and ghosts!'

Alfie sniggered. 'Where are you going now, Grandpa?'

'Oh, straight back to Werewolf Wood. Can you keep your eyes open for your cousin for me?'

Alfie nodded. 'Sure. I'll see you again tonight when it's full moon, Grandpa. Then we can search for Leo everywhere.'

'See you tonight, Alfie.'

Grandpa pulled his hat down over his face and turned his collar up so that only the glint of his eyes was visible. He looked left and right before walking out of the garden. His walking stick clicked on the paving stones. No one would suspect that the figure walking

down the pavement in the overcoat was actually a werewolf. Not unless they looked at his hairy black feet, at least.

Alfie watched him go, then walked back to the house. Suddenly a wind blew up, sounding like two voices singing a song.

> *'Rubbedy, rubbedy, rubbedy, rubbedy.*
> *Rub the last one out . . .'*

Alfie froze. Am I hearing right? he thought. Those voices . . .

He walked back to the gate and looked down the street. Leaves rustled over the pavement and gates banged in the wind. The street was empty. Grandpa Werewolf was nowhere in sight.

'That's funny,' Alfie mumbled. 'Grandpa doesn't walk that fast. It's as if he's dissolved into thin air.' Shaking his head, he went back inside. He felt bad, as if a boulder was pressing down on his heart. Three boulders, really. Somehow everything was going wrong. Arguing with Tim. Noura going to Luke's stupid birthday party. Leo missing.

And that wasn't even counting Chalker, Cheeker and Choker. He sighed. And now Grandpa Werewolf had suddenly vanished too.

27

Spying

When Alfie walked into the kitchen, Tim was sitting at the table next to Dad. Mum had put bowls of soup down in front of everyone.

Alfie was about to say hello to Tim when he thought, Wait a second. I almost forgot that I'm angry with Tim. We're having an argument. I wish we weren't, but we are. If Tim comes out now and says he's sorry, then everything will be OK again. As long as he's not embarrassed about Dad any more.

But Tim didn't say anything.

So Alfie didn't say anything either. He looked in the other direction and didn't sit down next to Tim. Tim shrugged.

'Dad, are you going into town to do some busking later?' he asked.

Dad nodded. 'It's late-night shopping so there'll be lots of people. I don't want to disappoint my fans.'

A smile flickered over Mum's lips. Alfie ate his soup silently, then pushed the bowl away.

'I have to go now. If you don't mind.'

Dad smiled. 'I know why, kiddo. It's full moon tonight. You go off and have lots of fun werewolfing. Give 'em hell.'

Mum rapped on the table. 'Take your mobile phone with you, young man. We didn't buy it so you could leave it behind. You never know when you might need it.'

The full moon was already vaguely visible in the sky. Alfie was hidden behind a bright-red Fiat that was parked across the road from Noura's. He couldn't stop scratching.

Werewolf itch. He always got it at full moon just before he changed.

He peered past the car at Noura's house and saw the door open. Noura came out, looked at a piece of paper and started walking. Alfie followed at a distance. The streetlights flicked on.

Where does Luke live anyway? Alfie wondered. It must say on that piece of paper. It's not nice of me to spy on her, he thought, a bit embarrassed. But I just don't trust this Luke character.

He ducked out of the way because Noura had stopped for a moment. She looked around as if trying to work out which way to go and every now and then she scratched herself too. Werewolf itch. Then she walked on. Out of the street, left, straight ahead.

Alfie crept from car to car. When there were no cars, he hid behind trees. When there were no trees, he hid behind hedges, keeping as close as he could to Noura.

Finally she stopped in front of an

old house. It was dark and looked very run down.

Noura pulled out the piece of paper and read it carefully. Then she looked back at the house.

Alfie had hidden himself behind a wheelie bin. He could see Noura frowning in surprise.

So Luke lives in that old dump, he thought. By the look of things, Noura can't believe it either. And why is it so dark? It looks deserted.

Noura walked up the path.

Don't, Noura, thought Alfie. There's something fishy about that house! Don't go up there!

For a moment Noura looked back, as if she could hear him thinking, but Alfie didn't dare show himself.

Turn back, Noura! he thought as forcefully as he could. Turn back!

Then the lights flicked on in the house. The front door opened. Warm yellow light leapt out on to the path and loud hip-

hop music danced out into the twilight. Voices. Party noises. A figure was standing in the doorway.

'Hi, Noura.' It was Luke. He brushed his stupid black hair back with one hand. 'Welcome to my party,' Alfie heard him say. 'I'm glad you could make it. Come inside.'

Noura followed Luke in and the front door banged shut behind her.

Behind the wheelie bin, Alfie groaned softly.

28

Come out!

Alfie blew on his hands. It was starting to get cold and he was still crouched behind the bin.

I'll just wait till Noura comes back out, he thought. Then I'll run straight to Werewolf Wood. She doesn't need to know I followed her.

He peered at Luke's house.

How long has Noura been in there? he wondered. Only ten minutes, I think. It feels like an hour.

He sighed, scratched his head and arms,

and then his legs. The werewolf itch was getting worse.

Just ignore it, he thought. Concentrate on Luke's house. There was a yellow car parked out the front.

It's almost as if I know that car, thought Alfie.

He looked up. The full moon was now clearly visible above the houses as a beautiful, white disc. It seemed to be smiling at him.

Alfie growled softly. He felt the cold moonlight on his skin. Hair started growing on his hands.

'*Wrow*, I'm changing already. Noura must be starting to change too.'

Now the hair started growing on his cheeks as well. His shoes started pinching. Alfie jumped up in a panic and kicked them off.

I'll look for them tomorrow, he thought. Noura has to get away from there. Come out of that house, Noura. Now!

Nothing happened.

Now! he thought again.

Then the front door of Luke's house opened.

Phew, thought Alfie. Noura's leaving just in time. She must have noticed.

He stared at the doorway, expecting Noura to emerge at any moment.

Too bad for stupid Luke, thought Alfie. We're off to have fun in Werewolf Wood.

But Noura still didn't emerge.

'What's keeping her?'

He peered over the bin until finally someone came out. And then someone else. Shrill voices sang a horrible song.

> *'Rub, rub, rub away,*
> *Rub the last one out . . .'*

29

Rubbedy, Rubbedy

Alfie couldn't believe his eyes. Cheeker and Choker came lurching down Luke's path with the rowing boat on their shoulders, singing their song at the top of their lungs.

*'Rubbedy, rubbedy, rubbedy, rubbedy,
Here and all about.'*

They carried the rowing boat over to the yellow car that was parked in front of the house and lifted it on to the roof, screeching away the whole time.

Alfie groaned. 'I didn't recognize the car without the rowing boat. What are those mad sisters doing here? How did they get into Luke's house? And why do they always have that boat with them? And where's Noura?'

There were far too many questions and Alfie didn't have a single answer. Cheeker and Choker climbed into the car, laughing

and cackling and calling each other names.

'Get in, witch.'

'Drive, hag.'

'Wa-ha-ha-ha!'

The doors slammed shut and a pitch-black cloud billowed out of the exhaust pipe as the car tore off.

Alfie looked at Luke's house. The door was still open.

For a moment he hesitated, then quickly crossed the road and ran up the path.

He tiptoed up to the door. There were no more party noises to be heard. It was silent inside the house. Alfie pushed the door open quietly and listened. Nothing.

He peered into the dark hallway. There was nothing moving. The house seemed deserted. As if there had never been a party.

Alfie whispered, 'Noura?' Very cautiously he ventured past the doorstep. 'Noura? Luke?' He took another step.

The party was over, that was obvious. But where were Noura and Luke?

Alfie went inside, his eyes adjusting

quickly to the darkness. There wasn't anyone in the hallway. Not in the living room either. Alfie's werewolf eyes saw a bare room with hardly any furniture. He could just see the dark outline of a small table.

'Noura? Luke?'

No answer.

'Wrow, this house is empty. There's no one here.'

He heard rustling behind him and spun around. His hand brushed something on the table, which fell to the floor with a bang. He felt something run over his feet: a mouse or a rat . . .

An enormous racket erupted. Loud hip-hop music. Voices. The dark, empty house suddenly sounded like a party in full swing.

30

Ghostly Noises

Alfie looked round in fright. Where were those voices coming from? And that music?

There was still no movement in the darkness. Alfie was getting more and more confused. Ghostly noises in an empty house.

'*Wrow*, stop,' he growled to himself. 'Don't panic.' He knelt down on the floor and felt around with his hands. After a while he found what he'd knocked off the table. A flat square box with buttons.

Alfie bashed it. *Click!* Instantly it was dead

quiet. No music, no voices, no hubbub. The silence hissed in his ears. Astonished, Alfie stared into the darkness.

'*Wrow?*'

Suddenly it was obvious. He didn't need any lights. It was as if a bright light had flicked on inside his head.

A recording, he thought. All that noise, the music, all those voices, it was all on a CD. Slowly, the terrible truth sank in. There had never been a party. Noura had been lured into the house with a CD full of party noises. By Luke! But why? Where was she now? And where was Luke?

Suddenly he saw it all in front of him like a film. Cheeker and Choker leaving the house with the rowing boat.

They've taken Noura away with them, he thought. They've kidnapped her. And maybe Luke too. Now I get it. It's not a rowing boat, it's a kidnapping boat.

31

Kidnapped!

Run!

Like a gust of white wind, Alfie tore through the streets. Leaves flew up. Cats leapt away from under his feet. Alfie ignored them and kept running.

'Wrow, out of the way, out of the way. Rush, rush.'

Down the street, turn right, straight ahead, turn left. Above the houses the full moon floated along with him. He rounded a corner, leaping over hedges and bushes. Finally he was there, leaning against a lamppost and panting.

He looked at the house across the road. Chalker's house. Where the two sisters lived. And Noura was here too. He was sure of it.

The yellow car was parked out the front with nothing on its roof. They'd carried the kidnapping boat inside, of course.

In the meantime it had grown dark. The moon was big and round. A crow cawed and took off from the roof gutter.

Noura's been kidnapped, thought Alfie. But where has that stupid Luke got to? Have they kidnapped him too? Serve him right. He shouldn't have lured Noura to his so-called party. It was his fault the sisters had nabbed her. Did Mrs Chalker know about it? Probably not, thought Alfie. She's changed an awful lot. The sisters were doing it secretly, of course. Mrs Chalker would bash them with her umbrella. But what were they planning to do with Noura?

I have to go inside. I have to warn Mrs Chalker. But how? I don't even know if she's

home. I can't ring the doorbell, Cheeker or Choker might answer. What should I do?

If only Tim was here. He always comes up with something. Wait! I'll call him.

Alfie pulled the mobile out of his pocket. Then he changed his mind. Oh no, we're still fighting. I'll call Dad instead. He's always ready to help.

Quickly he pressed Dad's number. *Tring . . . tring . . .*

'Come on, Dad, answer,' Alfie growled.

Suddenly there was a voice. 'Hello?'

'Hi, this is Alfie. Dad?'

It was quiet for a moment.

'No, this is Tim.'

32

Chalker's Clothing

'Tim? *Wrow,* what are you doing with Dad's mobile?'

'Dad's playing the Green Monster,' Tim said. 'Listen.'

The next instant the sound of the accordion was jangling out of Alfie's mobile.

'I'd gladly swap places with you,' Dad's voice sang.
'Or be a werewolf too,
Together we'd howl out a tune,
Under the light of the moon . . .'

143

'He's singing a werewolf song,' Tim said.

Alfie had to laugh for a second. Crazy Dad, he thought. Then he heard Tim's voice again.

'We're here in front of the supermarket. There are lots of people. I'm helping Dad. He's playing and singing and I'm going round with the tea cosy. I've already collected two coins and a button. Good, huh?'

Alfie felt his heart growing one boulder lighter. Tim wasn't embarrassed to be with Dad after all.

'Tim, we're not arguing any more, are we?'

'Course not, Alfie. But is something wrong? Where are you?'

Alfie was still staring at the house.

'I'm standing outside Mrs Chalker's house.'

'What are you doing that for?'

'I think Noura's inside.'

'Noura? Why?'

'I don't know. She went to a party at stupid Luke's. Those creepy sisters were there too. And now I'm here and—'

Just then the front door opened and the two sisters emerged, swearing at each other. They came down the path, got in the car and drove off.

'Alfie, are you still there?' Tim said. 'What do you mean? I don't understand a word you're saying.'

'No time,' Alfie growled. 'The evil sisters have just left. I'm going in.' He hung up.

Alfie looked left, right, then shot across the street and jumped over the hedge into the garden. There was a narrow path alongside the house.

At the back there was a big, brick extension with a badly spelled sign on the door:

CHALKER'S CLOTHING
Get you're free
clothes here if you're
childrens are paw and
under priviledged.

145

There was a dusty window in the door. Alfie pressed his nose up against it and peered through the glass. It was pitch black inside.

He tried the door handle. The door wasn't locked.

'*Wrow*, I can just walk in,' Alfie growled.

Suddenly he heard panting and hurried footsteps behind him. He spun around in alarm.

33

A Runaway

Alfie was standing with his back to the wall and nowhere to hide. Someone ran up the narrow path and came towards him. They stopped in front of him, panting.

'Alfie? Is that you?'

Alfie recognized the doggy panting and the raspy voice immediately.

'Luke?' Alfie tried to conceal the growl in his voice and kept his head in the shadows, out of the moonlight. He mustn't let Luke see his hairy cheeks.

'What are you doing here?' Alfie asked.

Luke was still panting. 'Long story,' he said. 'I'm looking for Noura. I think she's here.'

Alfie didn't answer at once. I'll act like I don't know a thing, he thought.

'Wasn't Noura at your party, Luke?' he said.

Luke nodded. 'Something went wrong. Noura was at my place, but then two old ladies suddenly jumped out and grabbed

Noura! They'd hidden in my house. The ugly old hags took her away in a rowing boat.'

'Kidnapped?' Alfie said in a whisper.

Luke tried to look at him, but Alfie kept his face in the shadows.

'Why didn't they grab you too, Luke?'

'I ran away,' Luke said. 'As soon as I saw them. I got out through the back door and hid in the bushes. I saw a yellow car drive off with the rowing boat on the roof.' He sighed. 'Then suddenly I felt ashamed of myself. I'd let Noura down. I'd been a coward. I started looking for her, street after street, house after house. Then I saw the yellow car in front of this house. So Noura must be here somewhere.'

They were both silent for a moment.

'And your parents?' Alfie said. 'Weren't they there?'

Luke gave a quick snort of laughter. 'I don't have any parents. At least, I don't know where they are. I live with my sister. And she wasn't home tonight.'

For a moment, Alfie was surprised. He didn't know where his real parents were either.

Weird, he thought. Luke and I have more in common than I thought. If his story's true, at least.

Luke looked at the door behind Alfie. 'She must be in there. Don't you think?'

Alfie nodded. 'You go first,' he whispered. His voice was getting growlier and growlier, but Luke didn't seem to have noticed. He grabbed the door handle and pushed the door open.

Quickly they slipped inside. Alfie looked around. It wasn't completely dark. The moon was shining in through the dusty window and the room seemed to be full of a blue mist.

'You see anything?' Luke whispered.

Alfie didn't answer. His werewolf eyes adjusted quickly to the darkness and he could already see almost as well as a cat. But of course he couldn't let Luke know that.

The next moment he had a tremendous

shock. Standing in front of him was a whole row of dark figures. Deathly still . . .

34

One Hundred Per Cent Werewolf

Alfie didn't move a muscle. Who were those people? Why were they standing still like that? It took a while for him to figure it out.

Of course! He was being stupid. They were racks full of clothes. Coats, trousers, things like that. Mrs Chalker's clothes for poor children. This must be her storeroom.

Just then he heard Luke's voice somewhere in the darkness.

'Alfie, where are you?'

'Here,' Alfie whispered. He stuck his hands

out and grabbed a couple of coats.

But his hands weren't hands any more, they were paws. And his ears were hairy and pointed. His nose had changed to a muzzle. Alfie was now one hundred per cent werewolf.

Thank goodness it's dark, he thought. Luke can't see a thing in here. But I mustn't let him get too close.

Quickly Alfie slipped in between two coats, the sleeves brushing against his ears. He stepped out on the other side of the rack. Yet another clothes rack was in front of him.

'Alfie, where are you?' Luke said. 'Wait for me.'

Alfie didn't want to wait for Luke and quickly crept on to the next rack. Again the pieces of clothing brushed over his hairy cheeks. Suddenly a hand grabbed his ear and felt it. Just for a second.

Alfie looked around in fright. There was nothing there except coats, overalls and jumpers.

'Luke, did you do that?' Alfie whispered. No answer.

'Luke?' Alfie searched between the clothes racks. No Luke. Maybe he got scared and ran away again, thought Alfie. He looked around carefully. The moonlight was making

strange things appear. There was a big black cauldron under the window for boiling the clothes for underprivileged children, next to the window was a big wardrobe, and lying in front of the wardrobe was the rowing boat.

Alfie blinked. Everything took shape and grew clearer. Suddenly he got goosebumps all over his body. Lying next to the rowing boat were a hat and a walking stick.

In that same instant Alfie was blinded by a beam of bright light. He screwed his eyes up. Someone was shining a torch in his face.

'*Wrow*, who's that?' he growled.

It was quiet for a moment, then he heard Luke's voice. Very loud.

'Quick, hurry. He's here.'

A door flew open and light shone into the storeroom. Two skinny figures with hats and umbrellas were standing in the doorway.

35

Men's Work

'Dad, pack up, quick.'

Dad looked at Tim in surprise. 'Why? Where are we going?'

'To look for Alfie. It's a strange story. Something about Mrs Chalker's house and Noura.'

Dad put the Green Monster in its case. 'That's funny. Isn't he with Leo and Grandpa Werewolf? It's a werewolf night, isn't it?'

'No idea,' Tim said. 'It doesn't make any sense to me either. But I'm still worried.'

Dad nodded. 'Me too. Mrs Chalker's not

a problem any more, but those creepy sisters of hers are.'

Just then the sound of a sheep blurted out next to them. *Baa, baa, baa!* Tim jumped with shock. Dad pulled out his mobile.

'Relax, Tim. That's Mum's private ringtone on my mobile.' He winked. 'Just a little joke of mine. Hello, honey, where are you?'

Mum's voice blared out of the mobile. 'I've finally found a broom. It's fantastic. A very good—'

'That's wonderful, dear,' Dad said. 'We're going to look for Alfie now. He's in danger at the Chalker house.'

'Pardon?' Mum said. 'What are you—'

'Sorry, sweetie, no time to talk. You just get back to your sweeping. This is men's work.' Dad hung up, looked at Tim and shrugged. 'This is not for women. Off to the rescue!'

Tim nodded. 'But what are we going to do, Dad? Those two sisters are really dangerous. They're not scared of us.'

Dad looked at Tim thoughtfully. Suddenly

his eyes lit up.

'I've got a plan. You remember what Mrs Chalker told us about her sisters?'

Tim thought back carefully. 'Um, something about them being scared of a monster?'

Dad smiled. 'Exactly . . .'

36

Trapped!

Too late, Alfie realized what was happening. He stared at the two figures in the doorway, who were holding their umbrellas out in front of them like swords. Their skinny shadows stretched out into the storeroom.

Oh, no, Cheeker and Choker, thought Alfie. I've been lured into a trap, just like Noura.

The bright light was still shining in his eyes. It was Luke, who had a torch trained on his face. Alfie held his paws up in front of him.

'*Wrow*, Luke. Why . . .'

Luke gave a mean little laugh and panted with excitement. 'You are one idiotic werewolf, Alfie. Did you really think I wasn't on to you? I can smell a werewolf a mile away. Just like your little girlfriend. Talk about easy!'

Cheeker and Choker came into the storeroom. They were carrying a plastic bag with something wriggling inside it.

'Well done, Lukey,' they cackled. 'We just popped out to the killer pet shop. Fortunately you were here to look after things. Now we've got them all. They'll make beautiful skeletons to add to our collection. The Rub Out Werewolves Club for ever!'

They walked over to the cauldron and upended the plastic bag. Something slithered into the cauldron. Now the sisters pointed their umbrellas at Alfie.

'Into the corner, werewolf. Fast!'

Alfie cowered back from the silver points of the umbrellas. He felt sick. So much silver! He brought his hands up to his throat.

'Ugh, I'm choking.'

Black spots appeared in front of his eyes and his whole body shivered as if he'd suddenly come down with a temperature. He stumbled backwards. Cheeker poked him in the ribs with her silver umbrella point.

'*Wrow-ow*,' groaned Alfie, grabbing his chest with his paws.

'Oh, poor little wolfie,' cackled Choker.

The sisters pushed him back and forth, as if he was a toy wolf.

'A werewolf for the cauldron,' Cheeker screeched.

'We've got the ugly four-eyed mutt,' Choker cackled. 'This'll be a laugh. Push! And in he goes . . . And then we'll leave him to our little darlings. He's all theirs. Biting, snapping, scraping him clean, until we have a beautiful white skeleton.'

The two horrible old women slapped their hands together and sang,

> 'We are two happy nasty crones,
> 'Cause soon we'll see some werewolf bones.'

They shrieked with laughter.

Alfie sat helplessly on the floor, half paralysed by the silver. What were they talking about? Who were their little darlings? Whose bones?

Just then the door flew open. *Creak-crack-creak.* Mrs Chalker was standing in the doorway. She shook her fist and stamped her foot. Her eyes spat fire.

'What's going on here, you horrible sisters? What are you up to?'

Never before had Alfie been so happy to see Mrs Chalker. Phew, he thought. Saved!

37

Revenge

'Well?' Mrs Chalker said. 'What's the story?' Creaking, she stepped into the room. Cheeker and Choker shrank. Mrs Chalker looked at Alfie, trembling in the corner.

Phew, I'm saved, he thought again.

'What did I tell you?' Mrs Chalker snarled. 'Are you disobeying me? Or are you deaf?' She jerked hard on Choker's earlobe. 'Do you want to lose another eye and ear? Just like before?' She raised her umbrella menacingly, pointing the silver tip straight at Cheeker's eye.

'No, no, don't,' the sisters moaned. 'Not again!' They held their hands over their lone eye and ear.

Mrs Chalker nodded. 'Good. You've got the message. Never start without me. I want to join in the fun.' She turned around to Alfie. 'So, little werewolf, I've finally got you in my clutches again. And this time you won't escape.'

Alfie looked at her silently. He felt as if his heart had stopped beating, as if his blood had stopped flowing, as if his breath was frozen.

'Ha-ha!' Mrs Chalker screamed. 'That's opened up your eyes. Struck dumb, aren't you? You didn't expect this. You fell for it. You thought kind-hearted Mrs Chalker was going to rescue you. Ha!'

Cheeker and Choker started to snigger. Luke was still shining the torch at Alfie and now Mrs Chalker pointed her umbrella at him too.

'Think again, wolfie. Kind-hearted Mrs Chalker doesn't exist. Only mean Mrs

Chalker. Furious Mrs Chalker. The bloodthirsty Mrs Chalker who only wants one thing. REVENGE!

'Because it was thanks to you that I got locked up at the RCUPA. Thanks to you and your family. That's why I founded the Rub Out Werewolves Club.'

Oh, thought Alfie. Now I understand. The R.O.W. Club doesn't have anything to do with people rowing. He tried to get up, but Luke pushed him back down with his foot.

'Stay!' he snarled.

'Attaboy, Lukey,' Mrs Chalker crowed.

Luke sneered at Alfie, who suddenly saw it all very clearly. Luke, pointing out Noura in the class. The strawberry cake with the silver fork. That was a vicious trick to prove to Mrs Chalker that Noura was a werewolf.

'*Wrow*,' he growled at Luke. 'I knew you couldn't be trusted. You betrayed Noura. I'll never forgive you for that. You're the most evil boy in the world.'

Mrs Chalker started laughing even louder. 'Boy? Is that what you think?'

Luke and Cheeker and Choker giggled along. Mrs Chalker nodded at Luke.

'Show him.'

'With pleasure,' Luke said. 'I'm glad to finally take this thing off.' He grabbed his face under the chin, just above his collar, then pulled it up, as if it was a peel. Alfie

growled with fright. All of a sudden Luke was holding his face in his hand. It was a rubber mask and the long black hair was a wig. Standing in front of Alfie was a small man with a bald head, a wrinkled face and beady little eyes.

'Meet my brother, Luke,' Mrs Chalker smirked. 'Bit small for his age and ugly as sin, but with a good nose for werewolves . . .'

38

The R.O.W. Club

Mrs Chalker stared at Alfie with a mad look in her eyes.

'You didn't see that coming, did you, werewolf cub? Luke is our little brother. We've been training him ever since he was a baby.' She sighed and seemed to drift off for a moment. 'Yes, those were the days. Before I came to live here. Beautiful memories . . .'

She blinked a few times and looked back at Alfie. 'For years we trained Luke and taught him everything there is to know about werewolves.' She picked at Luke's collar with a pointy fingernail. 'Luke was a good pupil. He's more obedient than Cheeker and Choker. As you can see, he's still got two eyes and two ears.'

A look of terror came on to Luke's face. Mrs Chalker quickly patted him on the head. 'Good boy, Lukey. Down.'

Luke laid his head on her shoulder and panted like a dog.

Mrs Chalker grinned. 'We hardly need to chain him up at all these days.'

'I— I thought you'd turned nice,' Alfie mumbled. 'But you're worse than ever. You're pure evil!'

Mrs Chalker looked down at Alfie. 'You think it was easy acting nice?' she screeched. 'It was hard work. It was disgusting, but I had to do it. Otherwise the RCUPA would never have let me go. I was released for good behaviour and I had to keep it up. I couldn't allow a moment's weakness. Like when you were hiding in my garden.'

'*Wrow*, you knew about that?' Alfie growled.

'Ha, of course I'd seen you. So I had to immediately switch to kind-hearted Chalker.' She sniggered. 'I think I did it quite well. I almost believed it myself. I should get a prize for it.'

'Ha-ha, a prize. Good one, sis,' screamed Cheeker and Choker, who thought it was so funny that they started leaping around and slapping each other on the back.

'And afterwards at that school with those repulsive children. And on the street when I bumped into you or your stupid family. I always had to be nice. Bah! It made me feel sick.' She bent over Alfie and started whispering. Alfie smelt her sour breath.

'But I stayed strong. My plan had to succeed. It was all for a good cause: Chalker's Revenge. Because of you, the RCUPA locked me up. That's something all werewolves must pay for. You're going to be exterminated. Rubbed out once and for all.'

'Yes, yes, revenge, cool!' Cheeker and Choker cheered. The R.O.W. Club for ever!'

'Shut up,' Mrs Chalker snarled. 'I'm talking. I want him to know exactly how I lured him into my trap. Let him sweat a little before he goes into the cauldron.' She pointed at the big wardrobe. 'You see that wardrobe? There's a surprise for you in there, wolf brat. A very big surprise.' She gestured to Cheeker and Choker. 'Open it!'

Cheeker and Choker raced over to the wardrobe.

'Really?' gasped Cheeker. 'Can I open it now?'

Mrs Chalker gave her sister a withering glare. 'Doesn't that one flappy ear of yours work? What did I say? OPEN IT!'

Quickly Cheeker pulled open the door. Two limp bodies rolled out of the cupboard and on to the floor, where they lay motionless.

39

Dead?

Alfie stared at the bodies in disbelief. They were bound tight with thick ropes, their eyes were closed and their jaws were taped shut with black tape. It was Leo and Grandpa Werewolf, showing no signs of life.

'Hilarious, isn't it?' Mrs Chalker said. 'Two dumb werewolves. But that's not all. How do you like our R.O.W. boat?'

Cheeker and Choker immediately walked over to the rowing boat and raised the lid, revealing a small black werewolf. Alfie gasped. Noura! She was lying completely motionless with her legs spread as if . . .

Alfie had never been so frightened in all his life. A shiver passed down his back from the top of his head to the tip of his tail. He looked up at Mrs Chalker.

'*Wrow*, what have you done? Are they . . . is she . . .'

'Dead?' Mrs Chalker sniggered. 'Of course . . .' She sniggered even louder. '. . . not. That would be a waste, wouldn't it? They're just knocked out, but they'll wake up soon. They still have to go in the piranha cauldron. After you, of course.'

Alfie stared silently at Mrs Chalker.

'Why the dumb expression, werewolf? Ah, I get it. You don't know what piranhas are, do you?'

Alfie kept looking at her without moving. I'm dreaming, he thought. This *must* be a nightmare.

Mrs Chalker giggled. 'All the better; it'll be educational, tee-hee. You'll figure it out. Because you're going in the cauldron.' Mrs Chalker gave a malicious laugh. Her eyes

seemed to have turned dark red.

Desperately Alfie looked around.
Grandpa Werewolf, Leo and Noura still
hadn't moved a muscle.

Mrs Chalker nodded to Cheeker and
Choker, who grabbed hold of Alfie.

Alfie wriggled and growled and snarled. 'Wrow, let go. Get off!'

But together Cheeker and Choker had a grip of iron. Their muscles were like steel from carrying the R.O.W. boat around. Effortlessly they dragged Alfie over to the black cauldron. Chalker pushed Alfie's head over the edge.

'Have a look, son. You're about to go for a swim.'

Dark shapes were moving under the surface of the water. Cold eyes peered up at him. The fish looked extremely hungry.

'Watch this!' Mrs Chalker shouted, sticking the point of her umbrella into the cauldron. The water boiled. Monstrous toothy jaws shot up, snapping. Mrs Chalker pulled out the umbrella again. The point was bent and covered with deep tooth marks.

'D'you see that, wolfboy?' Mrs Chalker whispered, panting with excitement. 'Did you see those big, razor-sharp teeth flash? My darlings can hardly wait. They're so keen to sink their teeth into you.' Cackling, she threw her umbrella down on the floor. 'Now it's your turn.'

They grabbed hold of Alfie.

40

Rescued?

Just then there was a bang on the door. A very loud bang. There was also a terrifying noise, an inhuman roar.

Cheeker and Choker looked at Chalker. They'd both turned white as ghosts.

'What's that horrible noise?' they whispered.

Alfie recognized it immediately. Maybe he was going to be rescued after all. Mrs Chalker was still holding him in an iron grip. Again there was a hard bang on the door: *CLANG!* Silence. *CLANG!* Slow and menacing, blow after blow landed on the door while the strange bellowing continued.

Cheeker and Choker hugged each other fearfully.

'Th-that's really scary, sis,' they whispered. 'It sounds like a . . . kind of monster.'

CLANG!

Even Mrs Chalker seemed nervous. Suddenly she stamped her foot angrily.

'So what? I don't care what it is. We're the R.O.W. Club; we rub things out. Anyone and anything that gets in our way. Even monst—'

CLANG!

The door flew open.

41

Unmonstered

There was the monster, looking very monstrous. It was big and square and long and green, with strange antlers protruding from its head. The monster howled, squeaked and groaned. Beams of light shone out of its eyes. Its snout was a long grey trunk that ended in scary tentacles.

Slowly, the monster staggered into the room. Its head rubbed over the ceiling. Its body writhed and seethed. It seemed to be moving under its skin.

Then it roared, howled and whined. Its

trunk swung through the air, grabbing at the old ladies.

Cheeker shrieked. Choker screamed.

'Help! It's the blood-drinking, bone-crunching cupboard monster. It's found us after all these years.' Trembling they crept into a corner and sat there hugging each other.

Even Mrs Chalker turned pale.

'It can't be,' she growled. 'I made up the blood-drinking, bone-crunching cupboard monster! Didn't I?'

The monster's shadow fell over her. Mrs Chalker stepped back, pulling Alfie along behind her. The monster swung its head, wrapping its trunk around her neck.

Mrs Chalker screamed with terror, fending off the trunk with one hand.

'Go away, monster!' She grabbed Alfie by the ears and held him in front of her as a shield.'

'*Wrow*, ow, my ears,' Alfie groaned.

'Shut your trap, werewolf!' Mrs Chalker screamed. 'Devour this wolf if you're so hungry, monster.'

'What monster?' interrupted a voice.

Luke stepped forward out of the darkness. He seemed to always hide in dark corners. Sniggering, he aimed his torch at the monster's feet. 'Look, it's wearing polished black lace-ups. Monsters don't wear shoes. Especially not shiny shoes.' Luke laughed. 'What's more, monsters don't wear tablecloths.' He grabbed the monster and tugged. A big green cloth floated down to the floor.

'*Wrow.*' Alfie tried to break free, but Mrs Chalker grabbed him by the scruff of the neck, squeezing hard.

'You're not going anywhere, werewolf. Look who we have here!'

The monster had disappeared. Now it was just Dad. Hanging from his neck was the accordion, which fell silent with a deep sigh. Tim was sitting on his shoulders with the coat rack on his head: the antlers. Above his ears were two thin torches: the monster's eyes.

PLOP. The grey trunk fell down. It was a vacuum-cleaner hose. The tentacles were a rubber glove, which now lay on the floor like a severed hand.

'Whoops,' Dad said. 'We've been unmonstered. That wasn't the plan. I shouldn't have cleaned my shoes.'

Cheeker and Choker emerged from their corner.

'I knew it,' Cheeker hooted. 'You're not a dangerous monster!'

Just then a loud voice roared out.

'Huh? Where be Leo now? Who the loony ladies?'

42

Strong

Leo, Alfie's big cousin, had come to and opened his jaws. Leo had very strong jaws and the tape had snapped immediately. 'Hey, why's Leo all winded up in ropeses?'

'Look,' Dad said. 'There's Leo. And Grandpa Werewolf and Noura!'

Mrs Chalker stamped her foot. 'Enough yammering! Grab those two fools and put them with the others. More piranha bait.'

Cheeker and Choker rushed over to Dad and Tim.

'Whoa, ladies, what are you doing?' Dad

said. He tried to push Cheeker away, but she was stronger. Choker grabbed Tim.

'Sorry, son,' Dad said. 'I thought this was men's work, but these ladies are super strong.'

Cheeker and Choker dragged them over to the cauldron.

Mrs Chalker's eyes gleamed in the dark. 'I've got a fun idea. First we throw the girl werewolf in the cauldron. We can all watch the fish doing their best on her. It will make a nice show.'

Alfie wanted to scream out, 'No!' But he couldn't get a sound out. Mrs Chalker had her bony arm wrapped tight around his neck.

'Luke, bring her over here!' Chalker said.

Alfie couldn't do anything except watch as Luke picked Noura up out of the rowing boat. He carried her over to the cauldron as if she weighed nothing at all. Noura hung helpless over his shoulder.

'Hey, what's the goings-on?' Leo shouted.

'What youse doing with Nourala? Why won't nobody speaks to Leo?'

For a second Alfie watched Luke carrying Noura, but then something seemed to explode in his head. He suddenly felt unknown power in himself. His blood surged through his veins.

'*Wrow!*' With a furious growl he broke free from Mrs Chalker, shoving her hard and knocking her over backwards.

'Ahhh, you rotten wolf,' Mrs Chalker screeched.

Alfie looked at her, growled and jumped on top of her. 'Stay still, you old bag! Or I'll bite your skinny neck!' Then he turned around. He looked at Luke, who was still holding Noura.

'*Wrow*. Put Noura down, Luke. Let go of her. You've already betrayed her once.'

Luke sneered. 'What you going to do about it, werewolf wimp?' He gave a panting laugh and wrapped an arm around Noura's throat. Under Alfie, Mrs Chalker peered sideways at the cauldron. Her umbrella was still lying between its black, iron legs. Carefully she reached out towards it.

Alfie glared at Luke, feeling the hair bristle all over his body. His whole being glowed with rage.

'I . . . I'll bite you really hard if you don't let go of her.'

Luke only laughed louder.

'Hey, somebody! Unpackify Leo,' Leo roared.

Mrs Chalker snatched her umbrella from under the cauldron and pointed the bent, silver point at Alfie. He jumped back with fright.

'Ha-ha!' Chalker screamed, pressing the point of the umbrella against Alfie's chest so that he couldn't move a muscle.

'We'll see who's boss around here,' Mrs Chalker rejoiced. 'Throw the girl werewolf in the cauldron. Now!'

Just then a shadow appeared at the window. CRASH! The window pane smashed into pieces, sending glass everywhere. Someone leapt into the room.

43

Women's Work

The moon shone in through the broken window, glittering on hundreds of pieces of glass on the floor. Someone was standing there. She was holding a broom.

'Mum!' Tim shouted.

'Darling!' Dad shouted.

'*Wrow*,' Alfie said in surprise.

'Yippedy-doodah,' roared Leo. 'Here's Mumsy. Set Leo free, Mumsy, quicks-a-daisies.'

All eyes were on Mum. She was wearing an apron, rubber boots and rubber gloves.

She had a tea towel tied around her head. She was holding her broom tight in both hands. She looked fearless.

'Time for spring cleaning,' she called.

'Ka-boom!' Dad said admiringly.

Mum summed up the situation at a glance: Tim and Dad held tight by Cheeker and Choker, Noura helpless over Luke's shoulder,

Alfie pressed up against the wall with Chalker's umbrella point against his chest, and Grandpa Werewolf and Leo tied up on the floor. She looked at Dad for a moment and softly shook her head.

'Men's work, you said? Tsss! This is a hopeless mess.'

Choker's arm was tight as a vice around Dad's neck.

'I'm sorry, sweetheart,' he gasped. 'I thought it was men's work. But there are too many treacherous women here.'

'Cut the chit-chat, will you?' Mrs Chalker snapped. 'This isn't a tea party, you know.'

Mum nodded. 'No, it's time for women's work. Girlpower.' Her eyes met Alfie's, who was paralysed with the silver point against his chest. She winked at him.

Mum twirled the broom in her hand and smiled menacingly at Mrs Chalker. 'You haven't changed a bit. You're as evil as ever. Once wicked, always wicked. Sad but true.'

Mrs Chalker burst out laughing. 'What

are you going to do with that broom? Sweep the floor? Be my guest, tidy up.'

Mum nodded. 'Well spotted. I have come to tidy up this mess. I'm going to sweep it away with my new broom. It's a very good one, I had to search hard to find it. The handle is made of the strongest Brazilian hardwood. The brush is real East African porcupine quill. And you've made a very big mistake.'

Mrs Chalker looked at Mum quizzically. 'A mistake? Me? What do you mean, Mrs Broom?'

Mum raised her broom. Light flashed in her eyes.

'You tried to hurt my family! My boys! That was an enormous mistake! Never underestimate an angry mother. Ever heard of broom fighting?'

'Broom fighting! That was it,' Dad mumbled to Tim. 'Mum's course. Not room lighting— Ugh . . .'

Choker was squeezing his throat. 'Shut up, boy.'

'Broom fighting?' Mrs Chalker laughed. 'Do you think that feeble broom—' For a moment she forgot to watch Alfie.

He knocked the umbrella aside and dropped to the floor, rolled over to Mrs Chalker and bit her in the calf.

'Oww!' screamed Mrs Chalker.

'Euw,' spat Alfie. Her calf tasted disgusting: tough and stringy.

Mum thrust the broom forward with enormous power. Right into Chalker's chin. *THWACK!* Mrs Chalker flew backwards, crashing into Cheeker and Choker and knocking them over.

Suddenly a cloud passed in front of the moon, blocking out the light. It was pitch black and everybody was yelling at once.

In the darkness, Alfie leapt at Luke. *'Wrow!'* He knocked Luke over and caught Noura.

Luke got up, swinging wildly, but missed everyone. He didn't have werewolf eyesight and could hardly see a thing in the dark.

Meanwhile there were hard blows. *BOOF!* *THONK!* Mum was going wild with her broom. Screams and yells.

'Ooph.'

The evil sisters started swearing. 'Shrivelled bunions! Twisted caterpillars!'

'Go for it, sweetie!' Dad shouted.

WHACK!

'Ow, that was me!'

'Sorry, dear,' Mum said.

'What be happening?' Leo roared. 'Leo wants to play too. Sets me free, please. Then Leo does some bashings too.'

Alfie dragged Noura to a corner and laid her down carefully, no longer paying any attention to what was happening around him. She still hadn't moved. Gently, he stroked Noura's coat with his paw. She has to wake up, thought Alfie. What have those demented witches done to her? She's lying so still. As if . . . Tears leapt to his eyes.

'Noura, wake up!'

She lay there motionless. She didn't even seem to be breathing. Alfie held his ear over her mouth and listened.

'Come on, Noura,' he whispered.

Suddenly Noura groaned. So unexpectedly that Alfie jumped. She opened her eyes. For a moment she didn't seem to be able to focus. Then she looked at Alfie with a terrified expression.

'Alfie? Help! Those scary women . . .'

44

Splash!

'*Wrow,*' growled Alfie. 'Hush now.' He had never felt so relieved. A raw sob escaped his throat.

'Everything's going to be fine, Noura. Mum's here.' He held Noura tight. She seemed to be only half conscious. Alfie rocked her gently.

'Listen, Noura.'

There was an enormous racket all around them. Objects flew through the air. Things fell over.

'Did you hear that, Noura? That's Mum

with her broom.'

They heard cries. 'Argh!'

And creaking. *Creak-crack-creak.*

Blows struck home in the darkness. *WHAM! BAM!*

The crash of glass. *RINKLE TINKLE.*

A door opened and slammed shut again. Then . . .

SPLASH!

Splash? thought Alfie. What's that?

Then it was all over and there was nothing but silence and darkness. For a moment.

Suddenly a sea of light flooded out of a small bulb hanging from the ceiling. Mum was standing next to the door with her hand on the light switch and her broom over one shoulder. There was a blush on her cheeks and she was smiling. She wiped a few drops of sweat off her forehead.

'Why didn't someone turn on the light sooner? Everything OK there, Alfie? And everyone else too?'

Alfie nodded and blinked, quickly looking around. He saw Dad, Tim, Leo and Grandpa

Werewolf. Everyone seemed to have come through it unscathed. Except for the big lump on Dad's forehead, at least. Tim winked and gave Alfie the thumbs-up.

Grandpa Werewolf yawned loudly, ripping open the tape around his jaws. He smacked his lips a couple of times and looked around in surprise.

'Where am I?' he growled.

'Youse be here, Grandpa,' Leo bellowed. 'And Leo be here too. We's both winded up. And now we's wanting to be unpackified, please.'

'I'm coming, Leo,' Tim said.

Alfie saw Cheeker and Choker lying in a pathetic heap in the corner, bony arms, legs, chins and noses sticking out at odd angles. Black and blue and out for the count.

Nice broom work, Mum, thought Alfie.

He searched around him. Where were Luke and Mrs Chalker? He couldn't see them anywhere. He looked at the door and the broken window. They must have escaped.

Noura turned her head from left to right,

stretched her legs and stood up gingerly. For a moment she wobbled. Alfie grabbed her arm.

'*Wrow*, I'm glad to see you back on your feet, Noura.'

Noura nodded. 'Me too, Alfie. What happened here?'

Alfie pointed at Mum. 'The short story is, we were all prisoners and Mum rescued us.'

Noura's eyes grew big. 'Really? Wow, cool. Your mum's a superhero!'

'She sure is,' Dad said, with a bright-red blush on his cheeks. He stared at Mum with an infatuated gaze. 'Darling, you're so . . . different. And you know how much I love things that are different. You're fantastic. I've never seen you like this before. You . . . you've swept me off my feet all over again. And that tea towel looks very cute.'

Mum smiled shyly. 'Sorry about the bump, dear. It wasn't easy in the dark.'

'It's nothing,' Dad said. 'It was just a loving little tap.'

* * *

In the meantime Tim had released Leo and Grandpa Werewolf.

'Where's my walking stick?' Grandpa Werewolf growled. 'And my hat?'

Alfie pointed at the R.O.W. boat. 'There they are, Grandpa. Over there.'

Tim picked up the hat and stick and gave them to Grandpa Werewolf.

'Thank goodness,' the old werewolf growled. 'Now I feel like myself again.'

Leo paced back and forth to stretch his long legs. He was more than two metres tall and still growing.

'Hey,' he suddenly roared, 'what be this?' He was standing next to the black cauldron and looking into it. 'This be full of floatsing bones and bitses. A whole skelly ton!'

Oh, so that was the splash, thought Alfie.

45

Who?

Everyone looked into the cauldron. Leo was right, there was a skeleton floating in it. They stared in silence at the gleaming white bones in the dark water. The piranhas were swimming around as well, looking as if they'd only just whetted their appetite.

'Who could that have been?' Dad asked at last.

Grandpa Werewolf growled angrily. 'I don't care. Not one of us anyway. We're alive and that's what matters. That means it must be one of the bad guys.'

Mum suddenly looked a little pale. 'Oh, heavens, did I do that? Did I knock someone into the cauldron with those ugly little fish?'

'Maybe, sweetheart,' Dad said. 'You were really going to town there in the dark. You had them flying through the room like ping-pong balls. Maybe one of them accidentally fell into the cauldron.'

Mum's gulp was loud enough for everyone to hear. 'I didn't know there were dangerous snapping fish in there.'

'*Wrow*, it's the evil triplets' own fault,' said Alfie. 'This is their murder cauldron for rubbing out werewolves. They wanted those horrible fish to chew on Noura's bones.'

'Really?' growled Noura.

'*Wrow*, sorry, Noura, but it's true. And afterwards it was going to be Grandpa's and Leo's and my turn.'

Leo growled loudly and kicked the cauldron. 'The scoundrelizers!' he roared. 'They almost exterminaterated us. Cuzwolf Alfie and Nourala and my old grandpa. And Leo too. To our bones and bitses.'

'So what I did was not really *that* terrible then?' asked Mum hesitantly.

Dad shook his head. 'Not at all, sweetness. It wasn't your fault. It was fate. They had it coming.' He peered into the cauldron again thoughtfully. 'But *who* had it coming?'

'Mrs Chalker or Luke,' Alfie replied. 'One of them ran off. The other one fell into the cauldron.'

They looked back at the skeleton. Dad shrugged.

'We'll never know who it is. Skeletons all look alike. A skull and a bunch of bones.' He shook his head and sighed. 'There's nothing we can do about it. But I've suddenly had a very good idea.'

'Really?' Tim said. 'What?'

Dad smiled. 'Shall we leave this awful building and go to our own, lovely house? For coffee and lemonade. And some nice, bloody steaks for the carnivores.'

'Grrr, yummy,' growled Leo.

46

All's Well?

They were sitting at home in the living room smacking their lips and sniffing and growling. Leo burped loudly.

'Urp. That was a yummilicious slabber of meat, Mumsy.'

Grandpa Werewolf licked his fangs and burped his agreement. Alfie and Noura had tucked in too. They licked the big plate clean, gave two quiet little burps, looked at each other and griggled. Dad looked sadly at the slice of cake on his plate.

'If only I was a werewolf as well. Then I

could eat a raw steak too. That's a lot cooler than a wimpy slice of cake.'

Alfie and Noura griggled again. Werewolves can't giggle the ordinary way.

'Don't moan, dear,' Mum said. 'I like you just the way you are. Not everyone can be a werewolf.'

Grandpa Werewolf nodded. 'Exactly. You can only become a werewolf if you get bitten. By a werewolf, I mean.'

Dad nodded. 'I know. What I was wondering . . .'

Grandpa Werewolf shook his head. 'Forget it. I'm not going to bite you.'

'That's not what I mean,' Dad said. He looked at Leo and Grandpa Werewolf.

'How were Cheeker and Choker able to catch you? You're big, strong werewolves and they're bony old pensioners. How did they do it?'

'Spray cans,' growled Grandpa Werewolf. 'Spray cans with silver dust. One of those grannies jumped out at me from behind a bush with a spray can in her hand and let me have it right in the face with a blast of silver dust. No werewolf alive could stand up to that.'

'Exacticiously,' shouted Leo. 'Those oldies sprayed Leo downside up in Werewolf Wood with their can sprays.'

'Me too,' Noura exclaimed. 'At that phoney party of Luke's. The two grannies suddenly leapt out of a cupboard. Luke held me tight while they sprayed the living daylights out of me. I blacked out completely and wasn't aware of a thing until I opened my eyes again. And there was . . . Alfie. My hero.'

A happy smile appeared on Noura's muzzle and Alfie's white fur turned a little bit pink.

'*Wrow*, Mum was the hero. She saved everyone with her broom.'

'That's right!' Dad cried. 'Let's all drink a toast to my courageous broom-fighting wife.'

'Yahoo!' yelled Leo.

Alfie didn't say anything. He was staring at Leo. There was something strange about him, but Alfie had only just noticed. His cousin was wearing a collar around his neck. A collar that looked familiar.

'*Wrow*, Leo,' he growled. 'Where'd you get that collar?'

Leo bared his fangs in a big growly grin. 'From that black cauldron. It was floatsing in between all those snappy fishies. Leo only needs to eat up one fishy. Then they let him take it out easily-peasily.'

Alfie looked at Noura and then at Grandpa Werewolf. He sighed. '*Wrow*. That means the skeleton in the cauldron isn't Mrs Chalker. It's Luke. It must be.' Alfie swallowed. 'Whoops, I remember something.'

He hesitated for a moment. 'I bit Mrs Chalker. In her calf.'

'Yuck!' growled Noura.

Alfie nodded. 'Disgusting. Just like biting into a piece of manky old leather. But seeing as I—'

Suddenly they heard a wolf howling in the distance. Grandpa Werewolf growled in shock.

'That . . . that's her . . .'

'*Wrow,*' growled Alfie. 'What a punishment. She hates werewolves and now she's turned into one. Because I bit her.'

'What?' Dad exclaimed. 'Mrs Chalker? *Her* and not me! That's not fair.'

'Sweetheart, stop going on about it,' Mum said.

Alfie walked over to the window and opened it. A thin cloud slid past the full moon. Again, a werewolf howled in the distance. It was a yowling, mournful cry. Alfie looked at Noura.

'*Wrow*, she must be so lonely now. I know how I felt at first.'

Noura nodded. 'But you had a loving family and good friends. She doesn't have any of that.'

'And it's her own fault,' Mum said. 'Come on, we've got something to celebrate.' She closed the window.

'Party time!' shouted Dad, who'd grabbed his accordion. 'I've got a new song,' he said and started singing at the top of his voice.

'Fun, fun, fun for all,
Werewolf party time . . .'

Alfie shook his head with surprise. 'Wait a minute . . . I know that tune. That's the R.O.W. Club song.'

Dad winked. 'Not any more, Alfie. The R.O.W. Club no longer exists. Now it's the Werewolf Club song. Our song!' He struck up the tune again, and this time everybody sang along.

'Fun, fun, fun for all,
In our party room,
We're the heroes of this song,
Especially Mrs Broom!'

Another

ALFIE THE WEREWOLF

adventure

Birthday Surprise

Alfie is no ordinary boy –
at full moon he transforms
into a werewolf!

It's Alfie's birthday and he's turning more
than just a year older. Something strange is
happening to him. First comes fur …
then claws … and then a TAIL. Before he
knows it, Alfie's a furry white werewolf!

He's going to have to get used to his new
wolfish lifestyle, and stay away from next
door's chickens … who knew turning
seven would be this scary?

Another
ALFIE THE WEREWOLF
adventure

Full Moon

Alfie is no ordinary boy –
at full moon he transforms
into a werewolf!

Alfie is on a school trip for two nights
of campfires, ghost stories and a spooky
outing into eerie Sulphur Forest.
The children aren't scared, but perhaps
they should be – something strange
is lurking amongst the trees, and what's
more ... there's a full moon
and Alfie's on the loose!

Another

ALFIE THE WEREWOLF

adventure

Silvertooth

Alfie is no ordinary boy – at **full moon** he transforms into a **werewolf!**

Alfie's happy days living with **Tim's family** are over when a **mysterious stranger** turns up. Soon, Alfie's **trapped** in a **cage** with a **grouchy vampire** and a **mysterious creature** called a **scoffle.** Will he find a way to **escape before** the scoffle **wakes up?**

Another

ALFIE THE WEREWOLF

adventure

Wolf Wood

Alfie is no ordinary boy – at full moon he transforms into a werewolf!

Wolf Wood has been home to generations of werewolves and hides an important werewolf secret … But when Alfie discovers plans to destroy the wood, the werewolves are in danger. Can Alfie save Wolf Wood – before it gets turned into blocks of flats!

Another

ALFIE THE WEREWOLF

adventure

Werewolf Secrets

Alfie is no ordinary boy –
at full moon he transforms
into a werewolf!

Alfie and his friends are on holiday.
A break from all the werewolf
mysteries and spooky
goings on? No chance!
When Alfie discovers a creepy
house, and a group of werewolf
children under the control
of a crazy lady, it's time to
investigate …